HORRIBLY HAUNTED IN HILLBILLY HOLLOW

BLYTHE BAKER

The ghosts of Hillbilly Hollow are whispering – and only Emma can hear them...

Emma Hooper thought coming home to small town life and the family farm would give her a chance to rest and recover from a traumatic accident. But that was before she started seeing ghosts. It was before Grandma Hooper started singing on the roof, and it was way, way before anybody spotted a ghost in a 19th century cavalry uniform coming out of an outhouse.

Can Emma learn to handle her newfound ability to see spirits, while figuring out a confusing relationship with the handsome local doctor? All while solving the ghastly murder of Preacher Jacob? Or is Hillbilly Hollow doomed to be forever haunted by a cold-blooded killer and a restless spirit?

CHAPTER 1

$\mathcal{S}$omewhere between the instant when I dashed out the back door at midnight in Grandma's nightgown and the moment when I found myself running barefoot through the muddy vegetable patch, chasing a frightened cow, it hit me. I was home again.

It wasn't exactly the cheery homecoming I had expected. I'd arrived late from the airport last night after a delayed flight, only to find that the tiny Missouri hometown I hadn't visited in years rolled up its sidewalks after nine o'clock. By the time a taxi I'd grabbed at the airport let me off at my grandparents' house, they were already dressed for bed. Grandma had stayed up just long enough to loan me a hideous nightgown and usher me up to my old childhood bedroom in the attic.

It was only early June, but the attic was warm, and I'd had trouble sleeping. I tossed and turned on the cot Grandma had set up for me, trying to find a comfortable position to get some sleep.

I felt as though I'd only been asleep for a few minutes when a familiar sound began to permeate my consciousness.

It sounded like traffic, like the blare of taxi horns and the shuffling of feet as hordes of New Yorkers moved en masse from street to street during rush hour.

Is that traffic? I had wondered in my half-asleep state. *How? Am I back home?*

I rubbed my eyes to bring myself out of the haze and realized I *was* home, but not my home in New York.

I stretched and scratched my belly, my fingertips connecting with a strange polyester fabric.

Right! My luggage.

I rolled my eyes, remembering that all my clothes, makeup, and other belongings were, at best, in a luggage hold fifty miles away, and at worst, circling the baggage claim at the wrong airport somewhere in the world.

I walked over to the window to see what the noise could be coming from below. I popped my head through the round open window, and looked down to see cattle – at least a dozen head – traipsing back and forth in the front yard.

"Well, sugar!" I exclaimed and clambered down the steps and out the front door to help Grandpa who was trying to contain the melee.

"One around the back! Take this." Grandpa casually tossed me a length of rope formed into a makeshift lasso.

Amazingly, I caught it and ran around to the back of the house where I hoped the unruly bovine hadn't trampled Grandma's vegetable garden.

Yowch! I muffled a faint yelp of pain as the arch of my bare foot connected with the sharp end of a twig sticking up from the mud.

I could hear Grandpa's voice growing fainter in the distance. "Hep, hep, hep, cows, hep!" His chant to round up the wayward cattle moved farther away as he herded them back to the right side of the fence.

"Come on girl, I'm not gonna hurt you. Come on!" I urged

and pleaded, but the thousand pound behemoth in front of me just looked at me blankly, uttering a noise that sounded more like meh than moo. *Meh...keep tryin', city girl, but I'm not budging!*

"Oh yes you are," I replied to the imaginary conversation.

I tried to toss the lasso around her neck, and missed. The giant black and white beast dipped her head, and started munching on the tall greens of a carrot plant. I made one more attempt to loop the rope around her head and lunged. She took a step backward and I fell, face-first into the mud.

As I pushed myself up onto my hands, a loud crunching in my ear made me look over. I was eye-to-eye with the wayward cow, who was now making short work of a giant, purple cabbage plant.

Grandma's going to be livid, I thought as I carefully reached for the rope that was now dangling from the cow's neck. Feeling victorious, I cinched the rope around her jaw and, standing, grabbed another carrot plant from the patch. I began to walk the beast back down to the pasture. I passed Grandpa on his way back to the house.

"I was comin' to see if you needed any help. Looks like you've got it all in hand, though." He tipped his chin at the cow who was now happily chewing on the tips of the carrot greens.

"Yep. I got her! Thanks, Grandpa," I said, pushing back a strand of my brown hair now caked in drying gray mud.

The dark eyes looking me up and down were older than mine, but the color and shape were the same. Now, they sparkled with a hint of amusement at my current muddy condition.

"Make sure you lock the gate properly. Have to be up in a few hours. Don't want to do this again tonight. I'll have your Grandma leave a clean dressing gown and towel in the kitchen for you. There's a bucket by the cistern. Don't be

3

trackin' that mud in the house now." He gave a quick wave with two fingers and headed back toward the house. "G'night, Emma."

Hmpf. "Did he seem impressed to you? I don't think he did. He should be. Catching you was no easy feat," I said to the cow as I continued to lure her along down to the pasture with the small piece of carrot still left in my hand.

We got to the pasture gate and I opened it, guiding the cow to the other side as I hung onto the rope. As I gingerly offered the tiny bit of remaining carrot with the tips of my fingers, I pulled the rope off from around her head with my free hand. I patted the beast on the head and she sauntered off, oblivious to the humiliation, filth and disturbed sleep to which she had subjected me. Watching the beasts moving toward the back of the grazing pasture, I wondered how none of them ever realized that they could easily jump over that low fence if they were so inclined.

As I shook my head and turned to head back to the house to clean myself up, I spotted something moving out of the corner of my eye. I looked down the fence line, in the direction of the little town in the valley below. If it wasn't two in the morning, I'd have been able to see the soft glow of the town lights. At this hour, though, only a few pinpoints of light emitted from that direction. The houses that sat on the outskirts and the closer ramshackle buildings like the old fort were completely dark.

I took a few steps, and looked back to where I thought I had seen the movement a moment before. I froze in my tracks as I saw it coming toward me.

Not again, I thought. *Not now! Coming back here was supposed to help.*

The pale apparition stopped approaching me and began to float down the hill toward the town. It paused, turning back, and waved a ghostly hand as if beckoning me to follow it. The figure was tall, wearing a dark colored coat and a wide-brimmed hat. There was something draped across its body from shoulder to hip.

I took a few more steps forward and the specter began to move away from me again and I realized it was moving toward the old fort, an abandoned historical structure on the edge of town.

I took another step, then caught myself, and stopped.

What are you doing, Emma? You're supposed to be here to relax...recuperate. You know perfectly well this is a side effect of the accident.

My doctor back in the city, Dr. Jenson, had told me that the apparitions were simply a misfiring of the electrical impulses in my brain – a byproduct of the injury I had sustained a couple of months before when my head hit the hood of a taxi that had struck me at a crosswalk. "Ignore the visions," the doctor had said. "Get some peace and quiet and they'll disappear in time."

I shook my head now, hoping the image would disappear from my sight. It didn't. Still, I was tired, and the mud in my clothes and hair was starting to dry and crust over. I needed sleep. I needed rest. So, I turned away from the figure and walked back up to the house.

At the side of the house, I found the cistern – the old hand pump for pulling water from the spring system that ran underneath our family farm. I pulled the upside-down red metal bucket from the top, and placed it on the paving stone under the mouth of the pump. I labored to pull the pump handle up and back down. It took three pumps before water came pouring out through the spout.

Yes! I've still got it!

I filled the bucket, braced myself, and dumped it over my head. I repeated the process three times, grateful no one could see me looking like a drowned rat.

I wrung out the polyester nightgown as best I could, and stepped carefully through the back door into what could, generously, be called the kitchen.

There, on the small table was a clean towel and a fresh nightgown. I peeled the still damp nightgown off and placed it in the sink, quickly grabbing the towel to dry myself off. I dragged the dry nightdress over my head, and wrapped my hair in the towel before going up to bed.

I spread the towel across the pillow, and laid my wet head down on it. The dampness of my hair and the towel cooled me down a little. As my eyes grew heavy from exhaustion, I briefly saw the apparition again in my mind.

Electrical impulses. A side effect. Nothing more.

I closed my eyes and my exhausted thoughts finally stopped churning, allowing me to find sleep.

CHAPTER 2

A sound roused me from sleep with a jolt, and I gulped in a lungful of warm air. I started to turn back over to go to sleep again when nature's snooze button sounded.

Stupid rooster!

With my face still buried in the pillow, I grazed my fingertips along the bare boards of the attic floor near the cot, looking for my phone. My hand finally hit the thin glass and metal form, and I picked it up, cracking one eye open to look at the time. Five-thirty-two.

I heard activity downstairs and knew Grandma and Grandpa were up, and probably had been for ages by now. I swung my feet around off the side of the cot and found the leather deck shoes I wore in from the airport the night before. I grabbed my phone, and headed downstairs.

"Good morning, Grandma," I said, kissing her cheek as I came into the kitchen.

The smells of sausage and fresh baked biscuits wafted through the air, bringing with them childhood memories of eating at the little kitchen table before school each morning.

7

"Good morning, Emma, dear. Sleep well?" she asked sweetly.

"Well, what sleep I got was excellent, thanks. Being awakened by cows in the middle of the night is definitely something I'm not used to anymore," I replied.

"Oh, I barely heard them," she said. "Breakfast will be ready in just a few minutes." She returned to the pan, flipping the sausage over.

"I'm going to run out back, then. Back in a few," I said, as I let the screen door slap shut and headed out across the backyard.

The Hooper farm had several structures, most of which were constructed nearly a century ago. The livestock barn was the largest, with a hay loft, and six stalls for horses, though we hadn't had any horses since I was a little girl. There was an equipment shed to keep the tractor and hand tools out of the elements, and a large chicken coop from which Grandma retrieved eggs each morning.

The main house wasn't much to look at – not much more than a shack, really. It had a sitting room, my grandparents' bedroom, a laundry room, a kitchen, and the attic. The kitchen had hot and cold running water, a luxury that I could remember being installed when I was very young. The laundry room, too, had water. The washing machine was a new addition since I left home, though it was at least twenty years old, and I had no doubt Grandpa had acquired it through one of his famous bartering deals. In the laundry room, there stood an old, claw foot bathtub. It had been there for as long as I could remember and apparently running water was added when it was piped into the laundry room for the washer.

Although there was running water inside the house, the toilet was housed in the original outhouse building. That, the

smallest of the Hooper homestead structures, was my desti-
nation as I headed out the kitchen door.

Still in the polyester nightgown, I walked through the
backyard, trying to avoid the still muddy spots from the
previous night's cattle stampede. Designer deck shoes and
cow-trodden mud did not mix, after all.

The outhouse was about fifty yards from the house itself.
It sat near the edge of the pasture, not far from the small
wooded area that began at the edge of the property.

I followed the trodden path through the yard to the edge
of the pasture, worn down from years of foot traffic to and
from the outhouse. Navigating the worn path, I was careful
not to scratch my bare legs on any briars.

Making it to the outhouse, I turned the wooden latch to
open it. I noticed a large, plastic reservoir on the back of the
structure that wasn't there before. It was open to the top and
had some sort of mesh over it. Once inside, I saw that
Grandpa had installed some creature comforts. Instead of a
box with a toilet seat fastened to the top, there was an actual
toilet – one from a boat or RV, by the looks of it, with a flush
pedal attached at the base. A garden hose with a spray nozzle
was poking through the back wall from the outside. I realized that the hose was apparently attached to the water
reservoir, making use of rain water to act as a form of water
for flushing.

Pretty ingenious, Grandpa!

As I began taking care of business, I heard a rustling
outside of the outhouse. It didn't sound like anything too big,
but definitely bigger than a squirrel or possum.

I finished up and managed the foot pedal flush and
garden hose setup without getting too much water on
myself. At the sink, there was an old coffee decanter with
water in it, so I turned the spigot to wet my hands, and

picked up the bar of soap from the dish. I held it up to my nose.

Mmm! Ivory!

The scent brought back early memories of having to wash my hands with a bar of Ivory soap using the little footstool in the kitchen after playing outside all day with Billy.

Billy Stone. I haven't thought about him in ages!

My mind flashed back to running through the pasture with my childhood friend, trying to catch lightning bugs in mason jars. I remembered us lying on the hillside at the top of the pasture, looking up into the starry night sky and talking about what we wanted to be when we grew up. He was my first crush.

I wonder whatever happened to that cute little boy next door.

I finished washing my hands and as I was drying them on the towel that hung beside the sink, I heard the rustling noise outside again. I carefully lifted the latch of the door, and opened it just a crack, peering out. I didn't see anything, so I opened the door a little farther, and to my relief, nothing was there.

As I swung the door open widely enough for me to pass through, I heard what sounded like a scream, and a small, white figure jumped into the doorframe.

Instantly, my thoughts leapt to the ghostly apparition I had seen beckoning me from across the field the night before.

Terrified, I stumbled backward, my back hitting the corner of the sink. A stabbing pain shot through my hand as it connected with the wall board. Wincing with pain, I shook my head to come back to my senses, and finally made out the small white figure as I heard another tiny scream escape its body.

Before me stood, not an apparition, but a tiny, white nanny goat.

"Holy smokes, you almost scared me to death!" I exclaimed.

The small creature's eyes met mine, and it took a step forward, bleating at me again, as if aggravated.

"And just what is your problem?" I asked. "I'm the one with a bruised kidney and a giant splinter in my hand!"

The goat stood fast, seemingly unaffected by my presence.

"Shoo!" I yelled. "SHOO!"

The goat shook its head and bleated again, louder this time.

"Oh, no. I'm not putting up with your shenanigans!"

I stepped over the small creature, and as I did, it leaned forward, and started chewing on the hem of Grandma's nightgown. The tug on the nightgown's hem caused me to trip, and I fell forward onto the dirt path. As I tripped, one of my shoes went flying, and landed in the tall grass. I stood up, looking for my shoe, and just as I spotted it, the goat snatched it up in his teeth, and began chewing.

"No! Stop it! Drop that shoe!"

I lunged forward, but the small goat was too fast, and leaped out of my grasp. It trotted down the path toward the house, happily chewing on my designer deck shoe. I chased it all the way to the house, and found it standing on the back porch, still chewing on what was left of my shoe.

Grandma opened the door to let it in just before I got there.

I burst through the screen door after the goat.

"Grandma, that thing has my shoe!"

"That," she said, pointing the wooden spoon she was using to scoop the eggs from the pan, "is Snowball. And if you didn't want her to eat your shoe, you shouldn't have given it to her. She'll eat anything, you know. Now sit down, Emma. Breakfast is ready."

"Grandma, I got a splinter in the outhouse thanks to this one's shenanigans," I said, crooking a thumb at Snowball. "What should I do?"

Grandma made a tsk-tsk sound with her tongue and teeth. "Sit," she said, retrieving a little, white, metal box from the cupboard. She grabbed the box of baking soda and set it on the table next to me.

"That's a deep one. Hold still, child," she said. She walked to the sink and put a small amount of water in a glass, then added the baking soda. She applied the mixture to the back of my hand where the splinter was, and put a large bandage over it.

"Leave it alone. It'll work its way out by the morning," she said.

She brought me a plateful of food, and a cup of strong coffee.

Looking over to Snowball, I saw that my shoe was beyond salvaging anyway, so I sat down to eat. I was famished from the late night arrival and the even later cow relocating.

"Oh, and your cell phone has been buzzing and blinking nonstop." Grandma pointed to the device on the kitchen table.

"Thanks, Grandma," I said, picking up my phone. I hit the button to unlock it, and saw that I had a missed call and a message. Seeing the toll-free number, I was relieved that the airline had called about my bag. I played the recording.

"Hi, this message is for Emma Hooper. Ms. Hooper, this is National Airlines calling about your bag. We have some great news! We found your luggage. Unfortunately, it was loaded to another flight, and is on its way to Vancouver. Once it arrives, it will have to go through customs, and be loaded onto another flight back to our hub

in Chicago before it can be sent on to Branson. As it stands, we hope to have it back by the end of the week. We'll give you a call as soon as we have an update. Thanks, Ms. Hooper."

Argh! I let out an exaggerated sigh of frustration.

"What's wrong, dear?" Grandma asked.

"Oh, it's my missing luggage. It's on the other side of the continent and I won't have it back until the end of the week. I'll have to put my clothes from last night back on and go to town to pick up a few things." I shook my head, and took a bite of the delicious sausage on my plate.

"Well, I washed your clothes this morning. They're on the line. Should be dry by this evening," Grandma replied, taking a bite of biscuit.

"Grandma, I have nothing to wear! I can't wear your nightgown all day," I said, appreciative that she was trying to help by taking care of me, but frustrated that I didn't have any of the things I needed.

"Don't worry, Emma, dear! I'll loan you something you can wear to town." She pointed her fork in the direction of Snowball. "Looks like you'll be needing shoes, too."

I rolled my eyes in frustration. "Thanks, Grandma. Hey, isn't Grandpa going to join us for breakfast?"

"Oh, no, he ate ages ago. He's out doing chores." She smiled sweetly at me.

After breakfast, Grandma put some clean clothes and a towel in the laundry room for me, and I bathed in the old claw foot tub. It felt good to get the travel grime and last of the mud from the previous night's escapades off of me.

I toweled off, raking my fingers through my dark hair as best I could to dissuade any tangles from forming. I grabbed the clothes Grandma had set out for me. They consisted of a turquoise blue sweat suit with a huge spray of pink flowers across the chest of the sweatshirt. She had also provided me with a pair of slip-on sneakers. Luckily, we both wore a size seven.

Slipping on the borrowed outfit, I tried to shake aside an uneasy feeling about the weird luck I was having so far on this visit home. Lost luggage, hungry goats, and creepy ghost sightings were the last things I wanted to focus on right now. I was under doctor's orders to relax.

CHAPTER 3

I grabbed my handbag, and took Grandpa's truck keys off the hook by the door. Before I headed out the door, I kissed Grandma on the cheek.

"I'll be back soon, Grandma. Do you need anything?"

"No, no, I can't say there is anything at all we need, dear," she replied.

On my way outside, I saw movement in the barn, and decided to go say hi to Grandpa before I left.

I walked out the screen door, and as I did, it didn't make the customary slam against the doorframe. I looked over my shoulder to see Snowball wriggling her way out the door behind me. She did a little leap off the porch, and trotted up to me.

"You're not coming with me," I said, to which she replied with a bleat.

Taking a few steps toward the barn, I realized she was following me. I turned again.

"I'm serious. You're not coming."

Again, she bleated.

I gave up and headed out to the barn.

The sun blinded me as I approached, and I couldn't see inside. As I stepped into the barn, and my eyes adjusted, I saw Grandpa raking up hay.

"Hi, Grandpa."

"Emma," he said, without really looking up as he continued his work.

I walked to the center post of the barn, and found the spot where my dad had carved his initials when he was a little boy. I rubbed my fingers gingerly over the spot. It always made me feel closer to him. I put two fingers up to my lips, kissed them, and waved them toward the sky. I had done that since I was a little girl. It was my way of sending my parents kisses in Heaven.

I hadn't seen my parents since I was the age Daddy had been when he made this carving. I was at the farm the night they died. They had dropped me off so they could have a night out. It was the middle of the night when the sheriff knocked on the door to tell my grandparents that their only son and his wife – my parents – were gone. A truck had taken a turn too fast. The driver swerved, and the trailer lost its balance. It was over quickly, from what the deputy told my grandparents. We went home and got my things, but from that point until I went to college, I'd been here, on the Hooper farm, with my grandparents.

My grandfather's voice broke my trance. "Emma," he paused, leaning on the top of the rake's handle. "Dorothy and I haven't seen you since you graduated college. That's been a lot of years. Not that we aren't glad to see you, but why are you here, exactly? Why now?"

He wiped the sweat away from the tanned skin of his forehead with the back of a gloved hand, and walked over to a hay bale, hoisting it over his shoulder the way a bodybuilder might pick up a barbell.

"Uh, well, I'm here to take care of you…and Grandma," I said, then realized I was talking to a fit, seventy-year-old man who was probably in better shape than I was.

It's not totally a lie. I expected them to be old. Feeble. In need of my help. Instead, they're active, spry, and healthy. In fact, I may be the sickest one here. It's doubtful either of them sees imaginary apparitions.

Grandpa looked at me quizzically.

Before he could say anything, a squad car pulled up to the front of the barn.

The driver's door opened and a tall, strapping, handsome man I didn't immediately recognize stepped out. Tufts of thick, blonde hair poked out from underneath the back of his sheriff's hat, matching his neat blonde beard. The man strode toward us, and called out to Grandpa.

"Mornin', Ed," he said. Then he looked me up and down, grabbing the rim of his hat, and tipped his head. "Ma'am."

"Tucker, what brings you out so early this morning?" My grandfather walked forward, taking off his work gloves.

Tucker? Larry Tucker?

I couldn't believe this was him. He was a few years ahead of me in school. He must have been thirty-three or thirty-four by now. Captain of the football team, and all-state baseball, he was always cute, and an amazing athlete, but it was well-known that the cheerleading squad had to do all his homework to keep him eligible for sports.

"Well, some bad news, Ed. There's been a death in these parts. A murder, in fact." Tucker said it more like a question than a statement. "We found Preacher Jacob this mornin' down at the old fort. Dr. Will's takin' a look now. No idea what he was doing there so late. You ain't seen anything strange, have ya?"

"Preacher Jacob? Oh, now that's a tragedy. A real tragedy. Who'd want to hurt a fine man of the cloth like him?"

17

Grandpa took off his ball cap, and clutched it to his chest. "No, no. I haven't seen nor heard a thing. I'll ask Dorothy, but she's been right here with me all morning. I just can't believe it." He shook his head. "Best preacher we've had. What a shame. What an awful shame."

"I appreciate it, Ed." Tucker turned to me. "Ma'am, you haven't seen anything unusual, have ya?"

"Tucker, I haven't seen you in such a long time. It's Emma – Emma Hooper. I was a freshman when you were a senior," I said, partly because I felt uncomfortable with a guy I'd known my whole life calling me ma'am.

"Emma? I thought you looked familiar. It's good to see ya." He smiled that megawatt smile down at me. "Real good to see ya. Sad circumstances, though, I'm afraid. You moved after high school, didn't ya?"

"Yeah, I went to college, then moved to New York. I haven't been home for…well, about five years, I guess." I blushed, trying not to look at Grandpa. I was ashamed it'd been so long since I've seen my family. I quickly changed back to the topic at hand. "It's a real shame about Preacher Jacob. I didn't know him well. But no, I haven't seen anything strange."

As the last word passed my lips, my mind flashed back to the spectral figure I had seen in the early morning hours as I closed the pasture gate.

"You-you said he was at the Old Fort? When do you think he passed?" I asked tentatively.

"Well, not real sure yet. Didn't look like much of a struggle, really. Dr. Will's down there now takin' a look at the body. He should be able to tell us more."

The radio on his shoulder crackled to life, and he mumbled some police mumbo-jumbo into it.

"Well, I best be headin' on. Lots of folks to talk to. Thanks again, Ed. Keep your eyes open for me, would ya?" He shook my grandfather's hand.

"Emma, good seeing ya." He stepped forward and patted my shoulder once, then headed back to his patrol car.

"Grandpa, I'm so sorry. Were you...were you very close with Preacher Jacob?"

I felt like hugging Grandpa would be a bit much in his eyes, but as he stood, wringing his hands and looking off distractedly, I felt as though I needed to at least try to be of some comfort.

"He's been at the church since Pastor Bailey retired. That's been, what now? Six, seven years? He was an important part of this community, Emma. Our moral beacon, and an active member of the historical society." Grandpa shook his head and put his gloves back on. "Course, you'd know that if you'd been around more, I 'spose."

I swallowed hard, my brow furrowing into a frown. Grandpa returned to his chores, and I turned and walked to the truck. He was right. I could have come to visit more often - checked on my grandparents more regularly. After all, this was still home.

I opened the door to the truck, and Snowball immediately tried to climb inside. I picked her up, deposited her on the porch, and using the most commanding voice I could muster, gave her a firm, "Stay!"

She bleated back at me, annoyed.

As I headed down the old gravel road from the farm, I looked over to the fence line where I had been the night before. I knew I'd seen Preacher Jacob before, but I couldn't picture his face.

Could that have been him I saw? Come on, Emma, get it together. It's pure coincidence, I told myself. *Just electrical impulses misfiring in your brain.*

I unconsciously put my hand up to my scalp. The knot may have healed, but whatever was still floating around in my brain, making me see things that I knew couldn't be there, sure hadn't.

CHAPTER 4

*L*eaving the farm, I passed Colton Road, and wondered how Suzy was.

Suzy Colton lived further down from us, but was my very best friend all through school. Her parents owned a large farm on the road named for her great-great-grandfather. We had shared everything together. Billy was my earliest friend, and we played together almost every day of childhood. When a girl gets older, though, she needs little girl friends. Together, Suzy and I ambled through adolescence. The pretty, spunky little blonde would boss me around, and I'd fall right in with all her hair-brained schemes. We were inseparable. We shared beauty tips, gossip, stories, and dreams.

My heart sank a little as I drove on. Suzy was my best friend my whole life. We stayed in touch for a while after we went off to college, but like so many things, over time, she fell away from me. Just like this place. Just like my grandparents.

I began to wonder if coming back was the right thing to do. I had only been thinking of myself when I made the decision. I needed a place to rest and recuperate, away from the hustle and noise of the city. Maybe I'd changed too much, though. Maybe I shouldn't have come.

I followed the dips and curves of the two-lane road as I got to the outskirts of town. The hilltop farms and pastures full of grazing cattle were scenic and serene, overlooking the town in the valley below. The view relaxed me a little.

I drove past the turn-off for the old fort. A sheriff's deputy had his cruiser pulled across the entrance with its lights on. A wooden board with the word "closed" in capital letters swung by eyehooks from the sign that marked the entrance to town.

I slowed down as I passed, and the deputy looked toward me and tipped his hat. I got suddenly cold, thinking of the man whose life had ended there less than a day before.

It was less than a twenty minute drive from the farm to this edge of town, but it felt farther.

I thought, *That's the difference between a New York minute and a country mile I guess*, and giggled to myself.

The town of Hillbilly Hollow itself was an idyllic slice of Americana. The place had another, more ordinary name once —Fort Harris, named for the old fort on its outskirts. But at some point, nobody could quite remember when, folk from the larger neighboring towns had dubbed the little settlement in the valley Hillbilly Hollow. Instead of taking insult, our townsfolk had embraced the name and begun proudly referring to themselves as "hillbillies" from the Hollow.

The town had grown a lot since those days but still remained one of the smallest in the area. The old fashioned main street looked like something out of a Norman Rockwell painting. I passed the shops and restaurants, heading toward the library and city hall where I knew the open parking area was.

My heart lightened as I saw the ice cream parlor. I thought of all the times I had begged my parents to take me there for ice cream when I was small, and of how Mom would always relent, saying, "Okay, Emma, just this once," with a wink. When I got older, Grandpa would pile Billy and me into the pickup, and let us pick up Suzy on the way to town. He'd give me three dollars, and we'd walk, arm-in-arm across the street to the ice cream shop for an ice cream and a pop.

I had no idea how long it would take for my luggage to actually arrive, and I needed everything. The general store would have enough makeup and toiletries to get me by, but I needed clothes and shoes that fit me properly and were more appropriate to a thirty-year-old than the sweat suit I was currently wearing. I looked down at the pink flower patch across my chest.

Blech!

At the end of the block, I saw a new shop that appeared to be a women's boutique. I pulled into the parking lot.

I stepped through the door of Posh Closet and found racks of sundresses and flowy tops, and bins filled with embellished flip-flops and funky jewelry. The shop was actually cute! I started flipping through the racks, and suddenly heard a voice from the back of the shop.

"Hi, there!" The voice bouncing between the racks as it approached me had an air of familiarity. "Welcome. Can I help you find anything?"

As the blonde woman belonging to the voice set a huge armful of clothes down on the counter and turned to me, I recognized her immediately.

She shrieked when she saw me.

"Emma? Oh, my gosh! I can't believe it!" She leapt at me, hugging my neck so hard she almost knocked me over.

"Suzy! You are a sight for sore eyes! I can't believe it's you! Is this your shop?" I asked, grateful for the warm greeting.

"Yes! I really cannot believe my eyes! When did you get here? How long are you staying?" She held my hands in hers, then looked me up and down suspiciously. "And why are you wearing what you're wearing?"

We both laughed.

"Very late last night, not sure, and the airline lost my luggage!" I replied. "Oh, Suzy, it's so great to see you! I'm almost glad the airline lost my stuff and I came in here looking for something reasonable to wear. This," I waved my hand up and down, "is Grandma's tracksuit."

"Yeah, no. Let's fix all that. Come on, I've got some things over here that would be super cute on you. So, what's it like in New York? Amazing, I bet."

She pulled several things from the rack, and showed me to a fitting room at the back.

"Oh, it's great! I just…" I paused, unsure what to say. I hadn't told my grandparents the real reason I was home, and I hadn't been gone long enough to have forgotten how fast news traveled in a small town. "I just came back to check on Grandma and Grandpa."

"I feel like they haven't changed in forever," she said. "Speaking of, have you seen anyone else since you've been back?"

"Well, I just got back late last night… Oh! But I did see Tucker at the farm this morning. Did you hear about Preacher Jacob? It's awful," I said.

"It is a shame. He was such a nice guy, too. Everyone liked him. I can't imagine anyone hurting him. Poor Prudence. She'll be inconsolable!"

I heard the familiar *vwoop* sound of a text message being sent from outside the dressing room.

"Oh? Were they together?" I asked.

"Oh no, honey, no they were not! Not for lack of her trying though! You know she's been playing piano at the church forever. I mean, she's not that much older than us, but hasn't she just seemed old forever? Anyway, she sure had a thing for him. She was always doting on him, and making him casseroles. Preacher Jacob is always…" She broke off, sniffling a little. "I mean, he *was* always trying to make sure he wasn't alone with her. Poor man."

I picked out three tops, a couple pairs of jeans, some t-shirts and a couple of dresses.

"Suz, can I just leave the jeans and top on? I can pull the tags off for you," I called to her over the door of the dressing room.

"Sure thing, hon. I think that's a good idea."

I heard the bell of the shop door ding, and Suzy told someone hello.

I stepped out from the dressing room with my purchases and the sweats draped over my arm. The jeans and button-down shirt I had on felt much more age-appropriate.

As I looked up, I saw a man leaning against the counter. He was about six-foot-three with ebony hair, and tanned skin. Dark eyes sat above sculpted cheekbones and a square jaw. As he stood up straight, his broad shoulders and narrow waist became even more pronounced. He turned to look at me and gave me an adorable grin that felt vaguely familiar.

"Suzy texted me that you were here, Emma, but I had to come see it with my own eyes to believe it," he said as he stepped forward.

"Billy? It can't be!" I hurried over and shoved all the items on the counter, and threw my arms up around his neck. "It is *so* good to see you!"

He picked me up and twirled me around.

"Great to see you too, Emma! I go by Will now, though."

He raised an eyebrow as he corrected me, part pleading and part warning.

"Dr. Will Stone, in fact! Well, he tries anyway, but he's still just Billy to us," Suzy added with a wink. "You know I had to text him the minute I saw you! Okay, let's do it!"

She stuck her hand out straight between us. "All…"

"For…" Billy added his hand.

"One!" I threw my hand on top of theirs and we repeated the order.

"One," Suzy said.

"For," Billy added.

"All!" I said placing my other hand on top of theirs.

We all laughed.

"So, you just roll into town and don't tell us?" Billy asked, wagging a thumb back and forth between Suzy and him. "That's not very good musketeer form, you know. What gives?"

"I'm sorry. It's not like that, really. I got up to the farm just after midnight. The airline lost my luggage." As I said it, I realized what a mess I must be. No makeup, scraggly pony-tail. Not exactly what I would have intended for a reunion with my bestie and the cute boy-next-door. "I just came to town to get some clothes, and everything I need until the luggage shows up. Speaking of, Tucker was at the farm this morning. He mentioned Doctor Will being down at the old fort. That wasn't you, by any chance?"

"One and the same, I'm afraid." He shook his head and rubbed his hands together. "Such a shame about Preacher Jacob. Such a great guy. It was definitely no accident, though. I'm certain."

"Really? So the rumors are true – it was a murder?" Suzy whispered the last word.

Small towns and gossip mills; some things never changed.

"I'm afraid so. I gave Tucker and the deputies all the

information I could. I'm not sure if it will help, but I'd sure like to see whatever lowlife did this come to justice." Billy's dark eyes flashed with a hint of rage as his brow furrowed.

I could see a bit of his father in his straight nose and thick, dark brows. Billy's father was half-Cherokee, and used to show us native hunting techniques, like how to walk so quietly in the woods that a deer wouldn't hear us, and how to fish with a spear.

"So, do you two musketeers want to get together for dinner tonight and catch up?" Billy asked. "Suzy, you think Brian can give you up for the evening?"

"Brian?" I asked, cocking up my eyebrow.

"Bailey," she replied smugly. "I'll be Suzy Colton-Bailey in October!" She jutted out her left hand to show a huge, sparkling diamond.

"Suzy! That's so great!" I said, hugging her neck. "Brian Bailey! Who'd have thought?"

Brian had gone away to college on a football scholarship and seemed destined to leave Hillbilly Hollow and never look back.

"I know, he was kinda smug in high school, but he really is a great guy. He came back a couple of years ago when his mom was sick. She's better now, but we ran into each other while he was here, and well, he just kind of stuck around. He's an engineer now, and travels a lot, but we make it work."

Her smile was beaming as she showed me her engagement picture.

"Good looking couple!" I winked at her.

"So, whadya say, Emma? Join us for dinner? How about you two meet me at the clinic about six?" Billy said.

Suzy looked at her phone and nodded her head. "Yep, I'm in. Emma, you're in too," she said, smirking.

"Still bossing me around, huh Suzy? Why start fighting it now? I'm in!"

We all laughed, and Billy said his goodbyes, before returning to the clinic down the street.

"I know, still so cute, right?" Suzy said, winking as she rung up my purchases.

"More than cute!" I agreed a little too quickly. "Did you two ever…" I gave her a look that finished the question.

"Oh gosh, no! Remember, Emma, he was your crush. To me he was more like a brother. I never went out with him. I dated in college, of course, and dated Ted Baxter – did you know him? Danny Baxter's cousin? Anyway, we dated for a few years, but it fizzled out after a while. Then Brian came back to town, I took one look at him and said, yep, he's the one."

She laughed, but I wasn't surprised at her sureness. Suzy always was the most together girl I knew.

I exchanged numbers with Suzy and told her I'd see her at six, then headed down to the general store.

Luckily, the cosmetics section there had enough to get me by until I got my luggage.

Next, I crossed the street and passed by Teller Antiques before popping into a little bakery called Sweet Adeline's, another new addition to Main Street. I picked up a dozen whoopee pies, and headed back to the farm.

The morning had started off grimly with the sad news of Preacher Jacob's murder. But with my plans for the evening and my sack full of pies, things were looking up a little.

CHAPTER 5

On the way back to the farm, I slowed down as I approached the old fort.

Missouri was a border state during the Civil War, with Confederate Arkansas and Tennessee to the south, and surrounded by Union states to the north, east, and west. Old Fort Harris was a Union stronghold, and as a result, was often the target of Confederate guerrilla raids. The fact that Union forces managed to keep the fort protected and standing throughout the war was a significant point of local pride.

The local historical society manned the fort, putting on Old Fort Days twice a month for tourists and locals from spring through autumn. The events drew large crowds to see the reenactors making soap, cooking over open flames, and putting on woodworking displays.

I studied the old fort as I drove past. I wasn't sure why, but despite the closed sign, in the absence of the patrol car, I decided to pull in. Something about the place just seemed to draw me there. I didn't pull all the way up to the main tourist

29

center building, but instead pulled just inside the brick perimeter wall.

The windows of the farm truck were rolled down, and I put the truck in park. I unbuckled my seatbelt and opened the driver's side door. I couldn't decide what I was doing there, or what I thought I was going to see, but I stepped out of the truck.

Looking around cautiously, I didn't see anything unusual, but as I took a few steps, a chill ran down my spine. It was almost as if I sensed an unseen presence hanging around the place.

Feeling unsettled, I immediately returned to the truck and quickly made my way back to the farm.

At home, I grabbed my purchases and headed up to the front door. As I crossed the porch, Snowball was still in the same spot I had left her earlier. She bleated as I walked past, and hopped up, following me to the entrance.

"Where do you think you're going?" I asked her.

She bleated again, and seemed almost to nod her head toward the front door.

I shook my head, and opened the door, and she trotted ahead of me into the house. In some homes that might have seemed strange, but Grandma had always had an odd habit of letting the farm animals wander in and out whenever they liked. She never seemed to mind cleaning up after them.

Not seeing any sign of anyone inside, I dropped my bags on the kitchen table, and headed out the back door toward the vegetable garden.

"Hi, Grandma," I said.

"Hello, Emma. How was your trip to town?" she asked, barely looking up from under her giant sun hat as she worked in the garden.

"It was great! I ran into Suzy, and then saw Billy. They

asked me to meet them for dinner in town so we could all catch up. I haven't seen them in forever," I said, excited to have reconnected with my friends.

"Of course, you haven't. You haven't been here, dear," Grandma replied nonchalantly.

She was a pragmatic woman. I didn't think she meant to hurt me, but her words made my guilt bubble up again.

"I'm so sorry, Grandma. I shouldn't have…well, I should've come home sooner," I replied.

"Well, I'm glad you're here now. Have dinner with your friends tonight. Enjoy yourself, dear. Young people should be with other young people. Besides, I have the quilting circle this afternoon. I was going to leave supper in the icebox for your grandpa anyway."

"Oh, quilting circle? That's nice, Grandma."

"Yes, I do like quilting. Though Margene Huffler does go on about her superior needlework. Fine talk for a woman whose first husband ran off with a cocktail waitress from Branson, if you ask me. Still, Maryann and Rose are good friends, and Diane and Ethel are fine, upstanding ladies," she mused almost offhandedly.

"Huffler…is that Prudence Huffler's mom?" I asked, remembering that Suzy had mentioned Prudence having a thing for Preacher Jacob.

"Oh, yes. Poor Prudence. She's a plain girl, but very sweet. Oh, and she had such a crush on Preacher Jacob, God rest his soul." She made a prayer sign and briefly looked upward.

"I imagine she'll be pretty upset about…you know, everything," I replied.

"Oh, yes. But Margene says that Prudence finally came right out and told Preacher Jacob how she felt and he shut that down in a hurry." She raised her eyebrow, but a small smirk was forming on her lips.

"So, was he seeing anyone, then?" I asked.

"Who, Preacher Jacob? Oh, no, I don't think so. He was a nice-looking man, mind you. Tall and slim…big smile, and a wonderful head of hair." She chuckled. "No, he was known to go out for a friendly dinner with some of the single ladies around town, but never Prudence."

"Hmm. Well, maybe they'll find out who did it soon," I replied. "I should get some work done, Grandma. I'm gonna go inside. Unless you need me, that is?"

"No, dear, go ahead and do what you need to do," she said.

I walked back into the house and pulled the box of whoopee pies from the bag and set the box on the back of the counter. I went up to the attic and put my bag of clothes on the cot. Then I retrieved my laptop and pulled my Wi-Fi hotspot out of the bag.

One bonus to being a graphic designer was the ability to work from just about anywhere. I started to open my email and decided to instead check out the news about Preacher Jacob's murder.

The local paper, *The Hollow Times*, had an article at the top of its website.

MURDER IN THE HOLLOW

LOCAL RESIDENT *and popular preacher Jacob Carter was found murdered this morning at the old fort. Sherriff Larry Tucker stated, "We are still investigating this tragic murder. We do not have any information to share on suspects at this time." The Hollow Times has learned that Carter, known to the local community as Preacher Jacob, was in the cavalry officer's uniform he wore for reenactments during Old Fort Days. The cause of death is not yet being released by police. Youth Pastor Danny Baxter will take over duties at Mount Olivet church. Carter did not have any immediate family. The church has asked that those wishing to pay their respects send donations in his name to the Hillbilly Hollow Historical Society, to which he dedicated so much of his time and energy. Service arrangements will be held on Saturday at the Mount Olivet Church on Main Street.*

I DID a quick online search and was surprised at how robust the church website was. The main page was a tribute to Preacher Jacob with photos, video clips of his sermons, and a memorial wall where all the residents of Hillbilly Hollow, at least all of those with internet access, had posted remembrances about the popular man.

I clicked on the link to a sermon he had given the previous year. The video showed a vibrant man, charismatic and energetic, walking from one end of the pulpit stage to the other as he preached. He was quoting from Hebrews, saying, "Keep your lives *free* from the love of *money* and be *content* with what you have!" He emphasized each word in the perfect time, punctuating each phrase with a fist in the air.

The parishioners were nodding their heads in agreement and applauding as he made sweeping hand gestures.

I saw Prudence Huffler starry-eyed and staring at him from the piano bench. I hadn't seen her in ages, but she had looked and dressed the same since she was a little girl. He looked in her direction at one point during the sermon and she literally clutched her pearls. It seemed to me that the word "crush" put it mildly when it came to Prudence and Preacher Jacob.

I clicked on another video, somewhat fascinated with

Preacher Jacob's charming smile and animated persona. In this video, he was playing with children at an Easter egg hunt on the church lawn. Something caught my eye and I paused the video, going back a few frames.

Is that...Mayor Teller?

As I recalled, our former mayor was run out of office some time back during a corruption scandal. There wasn't enough evidence that he was taking payoffs from a contractor to maintain city buildings to put him behind bars, but there was more than enough to have the citizens of Hillbilly Hollow vote him out of office. He now operated the antiques store in town.

In the video clip, Preacher Jacob was giving some money to a couple of teenagers who looked vaguely familiar. He seemed to be telling them to go buy more candy for the kids, since he was pointing to the basket of eggs.

What caught my eye, though, was Mayor Teller in the background behind him, leaning over to Don Polson, whispering something. Both men were looking in Preacher Jacob's direction with anger on their faces, and Mayor Teller was gesturing towards the church with his thumb. A moment later, the video panned away and I could no longer see them.

There was a link right below the video, so I followed it to the homepage of the Hillbilly Hollow Historical Society. The banner at the top was flanked by a photo of the old fort, and right below that was a welcome message from the Society President, Betty Blackwood.

I clicked on the link for members, and saw several photos of townsfolk in their reenactment gear. I gasped as I scanned to the bottom right of the page. There was Preacher Jacob in a dark jacket and wide-brimmed cavalry officer's hat.

Immediately, I shut my laptop.

No, no, no! It cannot have been real! It was just an illusion! Misfiring synapses!

I picked up my phone and dialed Dr. Jenson's office in New York.

"Hi, this is Emma Hooper," I said to the receptionist. "I really need to speak with Dr. Jenson. It's...well, I think it might be urgent."

"Just one moment, Ms. Hooper," the empathetic receptionist said.

I paced around the attic as I waited, and noticed a couple of cardboard boxes in the corner. I pulled a dust and cobweb-covered roll from one of them, and open it. It was a poster with an image of the Hollywood sign and the words Los Angeles emblazoned across the bottom. I opened another and found an image of the Chicago skyline. Realizing these were the posters that had hung in this space when I was in high school, I unrolled the third, knowing it would be New York.

You did it, Emma! I reminded myself. *You got out of this small town and made New York your new home.*

Now, though, I wasn't sure where I belonged. The big city had started to feel oppressive after the accident, especially with all the visions I was having everywhere I went. So then, I had thought Hillbilly Hollow was where I should be, but after seeing the ghost the other night, I wasn't so sure about that either.

"Emma, are you alright?" I heard Dr. Jenson's soothing voice on the other end of the line.

"Oh, Dr. Jenson! Thank Heavens! Listen, I took your advice. I came home to Missouri. I just got in last night, and I saw...well, in the middle of the night I saw...I had one of the visions we talked about." I sighed heavily. "I thought coming home was supposed to help!"

"Emma, you just got there. Give yourself some time. Remember what I told you. You need to reconnect with a simpler time, a more carefree time in your life. Do the things that you did when you were untroubled by the worries of an adult, and you'll find some peace. When you do, the visions should slip away."

His tone was soothing and gave me comfort.

"You're right, of course. I was just – I guess I was just anxious for an improvement," I replied.

"That's the problem, Emma. You are always rushing, rushing, rushing! Slow down, take it easy, and progress will come."

I could hear the smile in his voice.

"Okay. Thank you, Dr. Jenson."

I felt calmer when I hung up the phone. I decided to go for a walk in the pasture before I got ready to go meet Suzy and Billy for dinner.

I opened the door and found Snowball standing outside on the top attic step.

"Maaaah," she bleated at me, seeming annoyed at being left outside the closed door.

I rolled my eyes.

"Okay, come on!" I waved my arm and she followed me down the stairs.

I walked straight out back, past the outhouse and through the woods to the back of the pasture. I followed the fence around, and came back up on the far side.

I was standing near the gate where I was the night before, and I looked down into the valley. The scattered houses at the edge of town were visible in the daylight, and just beyond them, the old fort.

As I looked thoughtfully down at the place, wondering how someone as well-liked as Preacher Jacob might have met such a fate, I felt a thud against my shin.

Yowch!

I looked down and Snowball was at my feet. She head-butted me again, begging for attention.

I squatted down and scratched under her chin. She lifted her chin higher, and for a moment she seemed to be smiling.

"You're a cute little weirdo," I said. "Come on. Let's head back up to the house."

CHAPTER 6

*I*t was hot by mid-afternoon, and I helped Grandma hang damp sheets along the tops of the open windows and doors. It was an old technique, one passed down through the generations of farm families in the area, but it worked well.

"Gonna be a hot summer, Emma. Warming up this early, we're in for a long one," Grandma noted as we hung the last sheet over the window in the front of the sitting room.

She propped open the front door to let the breeze through more freely and I sat on the sofa to check my phone. I had one missed call from the airline.

Oh please, I thought, *please tell me you've found my bag!*

I hit the voicemail button.

"*HI, this message is for Emma Hooper. Ms. Hooper, this is National Airlines calling about your luggage. Unfortunately, your bag got held up in Canadian customs. It has cleared now, though, and we expect it to be on its way back to Branson tomorrow morning. We'll*

*give you a call when it gets in. In the meantime, if you need
anything, please give us a call at 1-800..."*

I HUNG up without letting the message finish playing, and let
out a deep sigh.

"Problem, dear?" Grandma asked.

"Oh, no. Just my luggage. It sounds like it won't be back
until tomorrow or the next day."

I sighed again.

"Well, at least you found some things to wear in the
meantime," Grandma said pragmatically. "Though, if you ask
me, Suzy Colton's shop is a bit overpriced. Of course, her
parents did always love a dollar!"

She shook her head, and I stifled a laugh at her love of
small town gossip.

I took a lukewarm bath, not ready to soak in a hot tub in
the late afternoon heat, and got ready to head to town. I put
on one of the sundresses I had bought at Suzy's, along with a
cute pair of sandals I had picked up. I applied the makeup I
bought, lining my top lids with a kohl pencil to make my
dark eyes pop, and brushed my hair to get the waves under
control before I headed out the door.

When I got back downstairs, Grandma had already left
for the quilting circle, and Grandpa was heating up his
dinner at the stove.

"I'm heading out to dinner with Suzy and Billy, Grandpa.
Can I bring you anything back?" I asked.

"No, thank you. I've got a fine dinner right here," he said
with a smile, and nodded.

"Don't forget I bought whoopee pies – the box is on the
counter if you want dessert. I won't be late." I started out the
door, and turned back, reaching up to deposit a kiss on the
deep lines of his tan cheek. "I love you, Grandpa."

"Alright, alright, go see your friends!" He bristled a little, but I saw the grin creep across his face.

I got to the clinic just a few minutes before six, and when I walked in, Suzy was sitting in the waiting room.

"Well, well, well!" she said, standing and placing a hand on the curve of her hip. "Don't you clean up nice? Billy's in the back. He's just lockin' up the good stuff before we go." She winked at me.

"I still can't believe you're getting married," I said, shaking my head.

"Well, it is what people do, Emma," Suzy replied.

"Not everyone." Billy's deep voice startled me as he walked through the area behind the reception counter, and closed the little half-door behind him. "Some of us don't get married."

"Not yet, anyway. You never know what the future may hold, Billy! You may find the right girl one of these days," Suzy said, elbowing him in the side.

He rolled his eyes and changed the subject. "Are you lovely ladies ready for dinner?" he asked, jutting out both elbows for us to each take one.

"You have *two* dates for dinner. What *will* people say?" I laughed, taking his elbow as Suzy took the other.

When we stepped inside the little restaurant across the street, Chez Jose, I was immediately impressed with just how nice and sophisticated it was.

Seeing the look on my face, Suzy immediately commented, "Come on now, Emma, we're not *that* backward around here, ya know! We do have a decent restaurant…now."

"No, it's just – I'm just…" I didn't know quite what to say to recover.

"Don't let her mess with you, Emma. You know as well as I do there wasn't anything this nice when we were kids. This place has only been here a couple of years. Remember Madeline Chouteau? She married a guy from St. Louis – Jose Ramos. Anyway, this is their place. Jose for him, chez for her, what with her family being French and all. He's a pretty good cook!" Billy said proudly.

"Chef, Billy, he's a *chef*," Suzy corrected him as the hostess walked over.

"Maddie! You remember Emma Hooper, surely?" Suzy directed an open palm toward me.

"Emma! How nice to see you! Visiting your grandparents?" Maddie asked, giving me a hug around the neck.

"Yeah, came back home to check on them and see how they're doing." The lie made my stomach clench.

"Maddie, hon, can we have a table in the back? Someplace quiet? We have *so* much catching up to do!" said Suzy.

"Sure thing! Follow me."

Maddie seated us and we spent the next three hours remembering old times, gossiping about everyone from our class and what happened to them, and talking about how our lives had been since graduation. As the evening wound down, Billy asked me the question I'd been dreading.

"So, Emma, how long do we have you for? You moving back for good?" He flashed that beaming smile of his. I always was jealous of his perfectly straight, white teeth. He hadn't had to suffer through braces like I did.

"I…I really don't know. I'll be here for a while though, I'm sure," I replied.

"Okay, kids, my ride is here. Gotta run," Suzy said.

We all stood up and Suzy kissed me on both cheeks.

"Call me. To-mor-row! I mean it, Emma. Don't make me chase you down," she said, grasping my shoulders in both hands. "And goodnight to you, *Dr.* Billy." She scrunched her nose up at him as she said it.

Billy and I walked outside and headed down the street toward his office, where I had parked.

"So," he said, "when are you going to tell me what you're really doin' here?" He towered over me now, and looked down authoritatively as if willing me to confess.

"What do you mean? I told you…"

But he cut me off. "Emma, come on. I've known you since before we could walk. I know when you're lying and right now, you're a big, ol' liar."

"Okay, but you have to promise not to tell anyone. Not even Suzy," I conceded.

"Musketeer pinky swear," he said, crooking his little finger and holding it up to me.

I crooked my pinky into his and we bounced our joined hands up and down three times, just like we did with Suzy when we were little.

"Well, I had an accident. I was in the middle of a cross-walk and a taxi jumped the light and hit me. I had a couple of broken ribs, and a few bruises, but my head took it pretty hard," I said.

"Oh, Emma. I'm so sorry. So a TBI? Did you lose consciousness? Open or closed? Any seizures?" He rattled off the questions as he appeared to be scanning my eyes for symptoms.

"Thanks, but we do have doctors in New York too, ya know." I laughed.

"Sorry, force of habit!" he said, running his hand through his hair. "But, seriously, you're okay now?"

"Yeah, it's just… Well, I'm experiencing some lingering effects. My brain sort of…" I paused, looking around to be sure the street was empty. We were in front of the library, so I plopped down on the bench, and Billy joined me. "I sort of see things sometimes. Things that aren't there. Or, you know, real."

I dropped my head and my hair fell forward. I cautiously looked at him from around the edges of it.

"Aw, Emma! It's okay! That happens to lots of people. I'm sure it'll pass. It's pretty common, actually," he said, patting my shoulder like he did when we were kids and I was upset about a bad grade or a stupid boy.

"I sure hope it goes away soon," I said, standing, and we continued walking back toward the clinic. "It's pretty disconcerting. Anyway, I came back to sort of recuperate. You know, take it easy, and get a change of scenery." I realized that saying therapist sounded a little too big city, so I said instead, "My *doctor* thought it would be a good idea."

"Sounds like a good doctor, if you ask me. Just as long as you're here, and I hope you're here for a long time, promise me you'll call me if you need anything. I'm serious Emma – day or night. Here, put my number in your phone."

I handed him my phone, and he put his number in, then dialed himself to save mine.

"Okay, promise?" he asked.

"Yes sir, Dr. Billy." I winked at him, and laughed as we approached the truck. "Oh, you don't have a car here?"

"Hmm? Oh, no. I live in town now. I bought the Johnson house up the street. I walked this morning. After I got back from the old fort, I just, I don't know, wanted to clear my head." He shook his head and shoved his hands into his pockets.

"Well, hop in. I'll drop you off. It's on the way," I said.

I grabbed the keys and opened the truck door, before climbing into the driver's seat. I suddenly realized how dusty and dirty the old farm truck was, but Billy didn't seem to mind.

"Wait, is this your grandpa's old truck? The one you learned to drive in?" He chuckled.

"The very same!"

I smiled proudly, remembering how expertly I had learned to navigate the behemoth.

Then a sobering thought struck me. "So, speaking of this morning, what exactly happened to Preacher Jacob?"

"Well, they don't want it out in the news, but he was strangled. Poor fella never saw it coming. It looked like whoever did it grabbed him from behind with the strap from a haversack," he said, shaking his head.

"A haversack? What's that?" I asked.

"It's those sacks the soldiers used to sling across their shoulders like this," he demonstrated, running his hand along his seatbelt from shoulder to waist. "Anyway, there was one not too far away, and it looks like they snuck up behind him, slung it around his neck, and pulled the sack through the loop end to make a sort of noose. Awful, really awful. Such a good guy, too."

"So, who do you think might've done it? You know everyone in town, I'm sure."

"Well, I know he fought like cats and dogs with Betty over some of the decisions she made on behalf of the historical society," he said, rubbing his chin with his thumb and forefinger.

"Betty Blackwood you mean?" I asked.

"Yeah, you remember her. She was our social studies teacher?" he asked. "But heck, she was old when we were little. I doubt she'd be able to hurt a fly, let alone a full grown man. I mean, Preacher Jacob was almost forty, but he was in great shape. Always did the fall fun run."

He thought for a moment. "And of course Prudence was crazy in love with him, but I don't think he was seeing anybody. I hear that she made some sort of declaration a couple of days ago. My receptionist's mom works at the church and apparently overheard the whole thing. Poor

Prudence. She might never recover." Billy shook his head as I pulled into his driveway.

"Wow, Billy! The place looks amazing!" I said, truly impressed with how the front yard of the old but beautiful home looked. Funnily enough, I used to joke with Suzy when we were kids that I would marry Billy and move into this house – the nicest one in town. I was half right, at least.

"Thanks. You should see the inside. I redid the floors and updated the kitchen. I even redid the bathrooms and put a steam shower in too." He puffed his chest up proudly. "You wanna come in and check it out?"

"Mm, it's kinda late, and my grandparents will be turning in soon. Next time though?" I asked, genuinely. I'd really enjoyed catching up with my old friends. I hadn't realized how much I'd missed them.

"Absolutely," he said, reaching over and putting his arm around my neck. I put my hand around his side to return the hug. "And don't worry, Emma, your secret's safe with me. Watch that noggin!" He smiled and hopped out of the truck.

"Goodnight, Dr. Billy," I yelled from the rolled down window of the cab.

As I drove out of town, I flipped on the truck's radio, and an old country song from the 90's began to play. I sang along to this blast from the past at the top of my lungs as I drove up through the hills, breathing in the country air.

I pulled up to the house and Snowball was waiting for me on the front porch.

"Come on, I guess. Let's go to bed."

I opened the front door and her furry little white tail wiggled back and forth as she trotted into the house.

Grandma and Grandpa were in the living room when I arrived, watching the nine o'clock news on the ancient tele-vision over an aerial antenna. I kissed each of them on the cheek and went into the kitchen to grab one of the pies from earlier. Then I plopped down between my grandparents on the worn-out sofa.

"How was dinner, dear?" Grandma asked.

"Good! Really good. Great seeing them. I didn't realize how much I missed everybody." I smiled, thinking of the funny stories we had told over dinner.

"You too, I'm sure," my Grandpa said without looking at me. "I mean, I'm sure people missed you too, while you were gone for so long."

"Maybe. But maybe people could've called and asked me to come home for a visit," I replied, still staring at the television like he was.

""Maybe people didn't want to be an imposition on your fancy, big-city lifestyle," he replied.

"Maybe people should know better," I said, and turned to him. "I should've come home sooner, Grandpa. I shouldn't have let work or being busy be an excuse. I'm sorry. I do love you, you know."

"Hmph! Well, you're here now, aren't ya?" he said.

"Like it or not, apparently!" I replied, giving him a huge hug and kiss on the cheek.

"Enough, enough already! Go to bed, child!" he tried to pretend he was annoyed, but I knew it was just an act. Well, mostly anyway.

"Goodnight," I said to them and headed up the stairs. Snowball followed me, and I decided to let her into the attic.

I put on one of the t-shirts I had purchased, and hung the bag with my clothes, my purse, and my carryon from various nails jutting out of the roof boards of the attic.

That should keep them out of Snowball's reach, I thought as I put my phone under my pillow and climbed onto the cot.

I was exhausted, but in a much better mood after having reconnected with so many people from my childhood. I thought about how grown-up everyone looked now. I still couldn't believe that goofball Tucker was actually sheriff, and Suzy was getting married to Brian. As I heard Billy's voice echoing in my head, I began to drift off to sleep.

For some reason, my last conscious thought was the memory of Billy's description of Preacher Jacob's death—murder by strangulation.

CHAPTER 7

hen I stirred, it wasn't yet daylight, but the early hours of the morning. I grabbed my phone from under my pillow and checked the time. Four forty-five. It was official. I was on farm time.

My mind was too active to go back to sleep, and I needed the bathroom, so I swung my legs around off the side of the cot. I rubbed my eyes, and found the sneakers Grandma had loaned me. Snowball opened her eyes and looked at me, but soon shut them again. I stood and stretched, which captured her attention, and she leaped to her feet and walked over to me. I scratched the top of her head and went downstairs.

The attic stairs opened into the back of the sitting room and as I descended them, I remembered that one stair creaked – the one I tried to avoid when I would sneak out to go bull-frog catching with Billy when I was little. I stepped around ol' creaky, and headed through the living room toward the kitchen.

With Snowball trotting along behind me, something brushed the front of my shin and I let out a yelp. I stumbled back, soon realizing that there were chickens in the house.

As my eyes adjusted, I saw it wasn't just one, but three, hanging out in the living room as if they lived there. I needed the bathroom even worse now, so I didn't stop to shoo them. Instead, I headed out through the backyard.

I used the outhouse and as I headed back toward the house, looked to my right toward the pasture fence. I turned, heading toward the gate where I had been the night before. When I'd almost reached it, Snowball stopped, bleating loudly, and lay down.

"What's your problem?" I whispered. "Come on girl." I put my hands on my knees and called her. "Come on, Snowball."

She made a little snorting sound and stayed put.

Emma, you're calling a goat like it's a puppy, I realized. *Get yourself together!*

I continued on without my companion, and as I passed the pasture gate, I was certain I could see a figure in the distance where I had seen something before.

A chill rippled through me. Still, I walked a little further down the fence line.

Misfiring synapses, I reminded myself. *Electrical impulses and that's all.*

I walked a bit closer, and could clearly see the figure of a tall man in the same dark jacket and wide-brimmed hat that I had seen before. I could see the resemblance now to Preacher Jacob.

My heart beat so hard I was certain anyone standing nearby could hear it. I took a few tentative steps toward the figure.

It moved nearer, then turned away, looked over its shoulder at me, and waved an ethereal arm, beckoning me to follow.

I took another tentative step, then stopped.

This is ridiculous. Ghosts aren't real, and if they were, why would the ghost of a man I barely remember having met want me to follow him?

I gripped the fencepost where I was standing.

The figure continued moving away from me, then turned back, as if it realized I was no longer following. The phantom seemed to point urgently toward the valley below.

No. NO! This is not real, I reminded myself. *I can't be seeing ghosts.*

I turned and half-jogged back toward the house. As I passed Snowball, she jumped up and followed me, apparently relieved I had come to my senses.

I returned to the attic and fired up my laptop and hotspot. I revisited the historical society's website and looked again at the photos from recent events. The image of Preacher Jacob certainly looked like the figure I saw in the field.

I stood and walked over to the round window at the pasture end of the attic. I cautiously peered outside. There was no figure standing near the pasture fence or anywhere else that I could see. I wondered if maybe the talk with Billy about Jacob's murder was simply invading my subconscious.

But, you didn't know about any of that when you saw the same figure last night, Emma.

Snowball ambled over to me and put her head on my knee for me to scratch it.

"Are you sure you're a goat and not a weird looking dog?" I asked.

She raised her head for me to scratch her chin and her ears went slack.

"Okay, little weirdo. If you're going to hang around me all the time, you're definitely getting a bath today. You smell like livestock." I giggled and had to put a hand over my mouth to suppress a full-blown laugh.

Wide awake, I decided to putter around in the attic. If I was going to be here for a while, I might as well make it cozy.

I pulled the New York poster from the box and laid it on the cot. I found a box that had an ancient roll of masking tape inside, and put it with the poster. I moved a few boxes and found a folding chair and a little table. I dusted these off and put them up near the window. In another box I found my old desk lamp, which I retrieved and set on the floor near the cot.

The last treasure I retrieved was the torn rag rug that Suzy and I made my junior year of high school. We used old t-shirts, a couple of Grandpa's worn-out work shirts, and random pieces of fabric stolen from Grandma's sewing basket. In truth, I was sure she knew we had taken them. We had spent hours sitting in my attic room, talking, laughing, and looping fabric through the holes of the rug pad I had picked up at the general store for three dollars. It was still in good condition and didn't appear to have much moth damage, but was definitely filthy. I set it by the door so I could take it downstairs and wash it later.

Returning to the poster, I made little loops from the masking tape and put it up on the wall across from the cot. All I had wanted when I graduated from college was to run off to the city. I would stare at the posters I'd collected and dream of the glamorous life I'd have someday.

But the tiny apartment I had shared with a roommate in the Flatiron district was certainly not glamorous by any stretch of the imagination. I had a cool walk-out balcony big enough for a narrow bench and a couple of potted plants, though, and it was a short walk to my job at the advertising agency. If I planned to stay here in the Hollow for long, I'd have to start getting some freelance work done, or sublet that place.

I walked over to the window again, and looked out at the farm and the pinpoints of light in the valley below. The sky was becoming lighter, a faint cast of purple starting to glow on the horizon. I took a deep breath and smelled the dew-covered grass.

I heard a noise from the rooms below and looked at my phone. Five-thirty.

I threw some jeans on with my t-shirt, and decided to go down and help Grandma and Grandpa with the morning chores.

CHAPTER 8

J walked into the kitchen and put on the coffee, nice and strong, just the way they liked it.

"Good morning," I said in a sing-song voice as they came into the kitchen.

"Well, look who's up early," Grandma said, patting me on the shoulder.

"Yeah, something woke me up, so I thought I might help you guys out," I replied.

"Pull that bacon out of the fridge, Emma. I'll go get the eggs," Grandma said as Grandpa poured a cup of coffee and sat at the kitchen table. He took a sip.

"Pretty good," he said. That was practically gushing coming from a man of few words.

I put the iron skillet on the large burner and turned on the fire. I pulled the bacon from the waxed paper and laid the strips out, close but not touching, in the pan. I pulled the long-handled wire screen from the hook about the stove and put it on top of the pan so the bacon didn't splatter, and popped a couple of slices of bread into the toaster.

Grandma came in from outside and deposited the basket of eggs on the counter.

"You might have more eggs on the couch. There were about three chickens in here early this morning when I went to the outhouse," I said, smiling.

"Oh, that would be Martha, Abigail, and Dolly," she said, smiling back. "They get nervous sometimes, and wander in.

"You're naming the chickens now?" I asked, cracking an egg into another skillet.

"Just the laying hens, not the fryers. That would be ridiculous," she replied, laughing.

"Ought to be glad she's just namin' 'em," Grandpa muttered, taking another sip of coffee.

"Here, let me take that," Grandma said, ushering me away from the stove.

I looked at my grandparents. They were definitely not the frail, dependent old people I had convinced myself I'd find when I got here. I had to tell them the truth – at least part of it.

"Listen, I'd-I'd like to tell you guys something," I started, sitting at the little kitchen table beside Grandpa so I could look at them both.

"Yup, we're listenin' I reckon," Grandpa said.

Grandma turned to look at me, occasionally turning back to the stove to check on the eggs.

"I didn't tell you the whole truth about why I came back."

"Knew that. So, what is it, then?" Grandpa replied, taking another sip of coffee.

"I was in an accident. It was a couple of months ago," I started to explain.

"Emma! You didn't tell us? Are you alright, dear?" Grandma asked.

"Yes, I'm – well, I'm mostly okay. I was crossing the street and got hit by a taxi on the cross-walk. I broke a couple of ribs, but had a really bad blow to the head."

I looked at them both. Grandma's face was full of worry. Grandpa was trying to remain stoic, but I saw the concern in his eyes.

"I had what's called a closed traumatic brain injury. Basically my brain bounced around in my skull. I'm fine, it's just that…well, it sort of messes with my vision sometimes."

Not entirely a lie, if you considered my vision including ghosts that didn't exist to be *messing with.*

"My doctor said I needed to get some rest. Maybe get out of the city for a while, so I thought I'd come back home for a bit. I really thought it would give me a chance to help you guys while I get out of the hectic pace of New York." I looked down at my coffee cup. "But, it looks like I was wrong. You… you don't really need my help at all."

"Oh, Emma! How could you have not told us about this? I'm very disappointed. Very disappointed indeed!" Grandma wrung her hands, then stepped over to give me a one-armed hug.

"Eggs, Dorothy," Grandpa said, and she rushed back to the stove to remove the fried eggs from the pan. "Hmph. So, you're gonna be alright though?" he asked.

"Yes, Grandpa, I will. I just need to take it easy for a bit. Have a little less stress," I replied.

"Stress! What a citified idea! Well, if it's restin' your mind you're after, I can put you to work for the day. Nothing clears the head like an honest day's work." He sipped his coffee again. "That is, if you think you can handle it." He cast his eyes subtly in my direction.

"I may not be farm strong anymore, but I'll try to keep up if you'll let me."

I felt a little better as Grandma set the plates down and we ate breakfast.

After we ate, I followed Grandpa outside and toward the pig pen. We spent the morning slopping the hogs, taking the tractor out to move hay for the cattle, and mending the back fence.

By early afternoon, I was exhausted, but feeling good about pulling my weight, at least a little.

"Grandpa, I was thinking I might get a mattress and put it up there in the attic if that's okay with you. That cot isn't very comfortable." I broached the concept carefully, not wanting to wear out my welcome.

"Might want to head up to McClain's down near Springfield. They're an honest firm," he said to my surprise.

"Oh? Oh! That's a great idea. Thanks, Grandpa."

I pulled out my phone and found they were open until seven in the evening. I could make the hour drive and be there with plenty of time to shop.

"I think I'll clean up and head that way now," I said. "Unless you need me for some other chores?"

"Nope. Go on ahead. I can finish up," he replied.

I grabbed my clothes from the basket where Grandma had put them after pulling them from the clothesline, and got cleaned up. As I was getting myself together to leave, my phone buzzed. It was a text from Suzy.

SUZY: U haven't called
    ME: Sorry! Was doing chores
SUZY: U R back home huh? LOL
    ME: Guess so! Heading to Springfield for a new bed
SUZY: My help is here 2day. Come pick me up on way

I WAS EXCITED to have my friend's company on the hour-long drive. I swung by her shop and picked her up.

She insisted on driving her Cadillac SUV instead of the old farm truck, and I didn't argue, offering to buy both the coffee and gas on the way.

We chatted on the drive down, gossiping more about people in town and the kids we went to school with and what had happened to them after graduation. I told Suzy all about New York and how it wasn't half as exciting as either of us thought it would be when we used to daydream about it as kids.

"So, Emma, you're buying furniture for your old room, now? Does that mean you're staying?" she asked, as we wandered around McClain's and I tried to determine if my thirty-year-old body would get enough support from a twin mattress.

"Um, well, for a little while anyway. Besides, if I come back to visit, I'd rather have a decent bed to sleep on. Oh – did I tell you I found the rug we made? I rinsed it out and hung it up on the line to dry. It's so cute – I'd almost forgotten about it!"

I decided on the pillow-top twin I'd been debating on, and waved the salesman over.

"You sticking around doesn't have anything to do with a certain cute doctor, by chance?" Suzy asked coyly.

"Suzy! What are we, seventeen? No way. We're just friends, just like always. But I have to say, I am kind of curious to find out what happened. With Preacher Jacob, I mean. I just can't believe one of our little town's residents is a murderer."

I checked Suzy's expression.

"Well, Brian and I ran into Tucker in the diner this morning and he asked if we'd seen anything," she said, running a finger along a sofa table. "Brian told him he heard Preacher Jacob arguing with Mayor Teller at his shop a couple of weeks ago. He was in there picking up a chandelier for his mom."

"Really? I wonder what that was about," I replied.

"He didn't know, but Mayor Teller seemed mad. That vein was sticking out in the side of his fat neck, apparently. You know how he gets." She snickered a little.

"Come on," I said as we lead the salesman out to the SUV with the little mattress. "I need to stop at a department store and pick up a few more things before we head back."

CHAPTER 9

*A*fter the drive back to Hillbilly Hollow, Suzy and I transferred the mattress from her SUV into the bed of the farm truck, putting my other purchases on top of it, and securing the whole thing with a couple of bungee cords I found in the glove box.

Back at the farm, I brought in the bags, planning to ask Grandpa to help me carry the mattress up. I opened the door to the attic, and Snowball preceded me inside. As I walked in to drop my bags on the cot, in its place I found a wooden bed frame. It was an x-configuration with a simple headboard and slats across it for support.

I dropped the bags and ran downstairs to look for Grandpa, finding him in the kitchen. "You made me a bed?" I asked, stunned and appreciative.

"Well, can't have you sleepin' on a mattress on the floor like a hobo. It's unseemly. You did get a mattress?" He raised an eyebrow at me.

"Thanks, Grandpa." I threw my arms around his neck.

"Come on, let's get it set up. Sky looks like it might rain in a bit."

We put the mattress on the frame and I was impressed that it fit perfectly. I had bought two sets of sheets, one I used without washing, out of desperation, and the second I put in the laundry room to deal with the following day.

I lay back onto the new mattress with its brand new sheets and pillows. It felt like Heaven in comparison to the cot I'd been sleeping on for days.

I'd swept the attic and gotten most of the dust out, and plugged in the little lamp, after clipping it to a ceiling beam. At the department store, I had picked up a metal clothing rack on wheels with a couple of shelves for shoes, which I put together after we finished the bed. I had also bought some field boots for wearing outside, and a few more clothes to wear for working around the farm.

"What do you think, Snowball?" I asked.

"Maaah!" she replied.

I started to get ready for an early night, tired from a day of chores and running around, when my phone buzzed. The text was from Billy.

BILLY: Good seeing u yesterday. Fishin 2moro at Ford's X. Wanna come?

ME: What time?

BILLY: Pick u up at 6?

ME: Sounds fun. C u then

I HADN'T BEEN to Ford's Cross since I couldn't remember when – high school, probably. We used to go there to fish and swim in the summertime. I was also excited to spend some more time with Billy. If I was honest, being back home and him not living right next door anymore felt a bit strange.

I decided I had better check my email and see if there

were any clients I needed to respond to. I spent a little time online searching for internet providers in the area, and wondered if I could talk Grandpa into letting me get satellite service instead of using my slow hotspot.

I heard a rumble outside and walked over to the window in time to see lightning in the distance. I stuck my hand through the round opening and felt the first few drops of rain. It was cool and refreshing against my skin in contrast to the summer heat, and I was thankful that the temperature outside seemed to have dropped because of it.

I went downstairs for a snack and a glass of tea. My phone buzzed again. Suzy, this time.

SUZY: Had fun 2day. 4got how much i missed u

ME: Me 2. 3 musketeers back 2gether

SUZY: All 4 1 and 1 4 all! Also I had brilliant idea. If u r sticking around a bit u should join historical society. Get you off farm and out a bit.

IT OCCURRED to me that Suzy might be a genius. The historical society would let me get to know everyone in town again. It might even give me the chance to put some of these nagging thoughts about Preacher Jacob to rest. If I could do that, maybe he would get out of my head, and out of my sight.

ME: Good idea. U r genius

SUZY: I know. Sleep tight!

I HAD the best night of sleep I'd had since I'd been home. The new mattress did the trick, and I didn't wake up until the sun was high enough to beam through the attic window.

I put on my jeans and t-shirt, along with my new muck boots, and headed downstairs. The smell of sausage and coffee hit me as soon as I reached the sitting room.

"Smells great, Grandma!" I said, as I grabbed a mug and filled it with dark, caffeine-infused, liquid Heaven.

"Sleep well?" she asked, pulling a piece of sausage from the pan and setting it on a plate for me, with a biscuit and some fried potatoes.

"Yep. Any idea where Grandpa is this morning? I thought I could help him with some chores before I head to town."

"He was headed down to the equipment shed, last I saw. Think he plans to work on the tractor. I could use some help with the garden, though, and I have a little canning to do this morning as well." She looked up at me as if to see if I would take the hint.

"Oh, I'd love to help with that!" I replied.

We spent the next couple of hours tending to the vegetable patch that was in the backyard behind the farmhouse. Grandpa grew soybeans, corn, and cotton on the farm, and kept a field for hay. He had cows, pigs, chickens, a handful of goats, and a substantial beehive in the back pasture. Grandma's garden, though, was really just for the household. She grew tomatoes, okra, cucumbers for pickles, carrots, and green beans. She added watermelon, pumpkins, and squash in season. On this particular day, she wanted to can the tomatoes that were at the peak of flavor just about now.

We brought the tomatoes inside and spent the next three hours prepping and canning them. I didn't seem to have the knack for blanching them long enough for the skins to slough off, so she put me on table duty, cutting the tomatoes up to transfer into the large pot.

"This would be so much easier with an immersion blender, Grandma. I'd be happy to pick one up for you."

I knew they could afford things like appliances, dryers, and new televisions, probably better than I could. Still, they were famously frugal. *Make it do or do without!* Grandma was fond of saying.

"Emma! I don't need some new-fangled gadgets to get my work done! Gracious me!" She shook her head and made a tsk-tsk sound between her tongue and teeth.

We saved back a few of the ripe tomatoes, and Grandma sliced one onto a plate, sprinkling it with just a little salt.

"Here you are! Nothing finer than a summer tomato, fresh from the garden!" she said.

She put the plate on the table and we gobbled up most of the slices, though I did slip one or two to Snowball, who was sitting between my feet waiting for her chance to swoop in and steal one.

After we finished in the kitchen, I cleaned myself up and headed to town. I decided to stop by and see Suzy before I headed over to the historical society to volunteer.

"What's new, Suzy Q?" I asked as I entered the shop.

"Please, don't," she said, rolling her eyes at the greeting. "Not much. Slow today. What are you doing in town?" she asked.

"I'm heading over to the historical society. I thought your idea was great – get me out of the house a bit, and the old fort weekends sound kinda fun!"

I plopped down on the stool behind the counter next to Suzy and we started chatting. The bell on the shop door rang, and Tucker walked in with a folder in his hand.

"Suzy." He tipped his hat to her, then me. "Emma. I was hopin' I could put one of these flyers up in your window there. Historical society has ponied up a little incentive for anybody who knows anything 'bout Preacher Jacob's murder to come forward," he said, one dark blonde eyebrow jutting up as he took off his sunglasses and tucked the arm through the open top button hole of his shirt.

"Sure, Tucker, I'd be happy to put it up if you give me one," Suzy replied.

"So, no leads then?" I asked hesitantly.

"No, not yet. Darndest thing. No idea what he was doin' at the old fort that time o' night, and in his cavalry uniform too. Mighty strange thing," he said, mindlessly rubbing the whiskers of his beard with his thumb and forefingers as he pursed his lips. "Anyway, I appreciate it, Suzy. And you heard the candlelight vigil is tomorrow night at the church, right? Service is on Saturday. You two ladies be safe out there."

He tipped his hat to the pair of us, donned his shades and stepped back out onto the sidewalk.

"Weird that he grew up to be so..." I started.

"Crazy handsome? Yeah!" Suzy said.

"But he still seems awfully..."

Again, she interrupted me. "Dumb as a box of rocks? 'Fraid so!"

We both laughed hysterically.

I said goodbye to Suzy as she posted the flyer in the window of the shop.

As I walked down Main Street, all the other businesses had the same flyer in their windows as well.

REWARD: $1000 for information leading to the capture and conviction of the person or persons responsible for the death of Preacher Jacob Carter, clergyman, and beloved member of the Hill-billy Hollow Historical Society. Anyone with information should call the Sheriff's Department Tip Line at...

I WALKED past Billy's clinic and the church, the front lawn of which was covered in bundles of flowers, wreaths, candles, and cards, all memorializing Preacher Jacob.

A crayon drawing caught my eye, and I stopped to look more closely. It showed a small girl with an Easter basket, and a man in a wide-brimmed dark hat holding her hand. A yellow oval was drawn above the man's hat, like a halo, and a cross was drawn in the upper corner. The child who had drawn it couldn't be older than five or six.

I put my hand to my heart.

Wow, people are really going to miss him!

I continued on the two blocks to the Hillbilly Hollow Historical Society building at the corner of Main and Maple Street.

"Hello," I said to the woman behind the counter as I walked in.

"Afternoon. Can I help you?" she replied.

She looked over her glasses at me; they had a silver chain attached to them that snaked behind her neck. The glasses combined with the tightly wound bun atop her head reminded me of a school headmistress from an old movie. The woman was probably in her fifties, and her face looked vaguely familiar but I couldn't quite place it.

"Yes. Hi. Um, I'd...I'd like to join the historical society?" Her commanding presence made me say it as a question.

"Is that...are you the Hooper girl?" she asked, after studying my face for a moment.

"Yes, ma'am. Emma Hooper. I'm sorry – I know we know each other, but I can't quite place..." I began to apologize.

"Sadie Cooper! Remember? I used to work at the elementary school? I haven't seen you in forever. Heard you moved off to New York or some such!" she said, shaking her head.

"Oh, I did after college. But I'm back now." I forced a small smile. I vaguely remembered Ms. Cooper. I thought her son was a few years ahead of me in school. She had been widowed before I moved away.

"Well, let me go see if Betty's free. Have a seat right over here. I'll be right back."

She sauntered off into the only office in the place and returned a moment later.

"Come on back, hon!"

The Hillbilly Hollow Historical Society was in a tiny storefront at the end of a strip of businesses on Main Street. It had a small reception area with a counter and several chairs, a water fountain, and a few shelves full of books, maps, and knick-knacks emblazoned with the *Hillbilly Hollow* name. Behind the counter was a small open work space with a copier and a file cabinet, and beyond that was a small office, a conference room that might hold about twenty people, and a restroom.

I followed Sadie into the small office with *Office of the President* emblazoned on the door.

The desk in the small room was far too big and grand for the space, and there were two little wooden chairs opposite the desk with leatherette upholstered seats. The wall behind the desk was crammed full of plaques and photos of events at the old fort over the years, some of which appeared quite old. I recognized the former president of the historical society, Buzz Dodson, in some of the photos. The ones in the most prominent and eye-catching spots on the wall all featured the current president, who was sitting behind the desk as I walked in.

"Hello, Emma," Betty Blackwood said as I entered. "Please have a seat."

Betty's hair was even grayer than I remembered. She was wearing a Chanel-style jacket in a dark pink woven fabric with cream trim and gold buttons.

Very presidential, indeed, I thought as I sat down.

"So good to see you, Mrs. Blackwood," I replied. "I was so sorry to hear about your loss." I looked at her sympathetically.

"My what?" she asked, seeming to have no idea what I meant.

"Well, I mean, Preacher Jacob. He was a member, wasn't he?"

"Oh, that! Yes, yes, very tragic." She waved a hand in the air dismissively as she said it. "However, Sadie tells me you're interested in joining the society, and we *have* had a spot recently come open."

Ouch! That's pretty cold, I thought as she tried to suppress a grin.

"Well, yes. I'd like to volunteer. I think it would help me reconnect with the town – you know, get back to my roots. Besides, I think that Old Fort Days sound like a lot of fun!"

I smiled at this last part and was unexpectedly met with a stern look from Betty.

"Old Fort Days are serious business." She pointed a crooked finger in the air for emphasis. "Serious business indeed! Do you know how much money those weekends bring in to the historical society? Do you have any idea the costs associated with maintaining the old fort? This office? The grounds, the electricity… Well, it just goes on and on!"

She seemed to have gone off into her own world, and wasn't talking to me so much as ranting.

"At any rate, *some* people don't seem to understand how important that revenue is to the old fort…to *our* town!" She looked at me, eyes wide, with a wrinkle high in her brow.

"Mrs. Blackwood, I just meant to say that bringing history to life is fun for our visitors, and I would really enjoy being able to share our heritage with them." I mustered my most charming smile.

Blinking, she replied, "Yes, of course! Of course! We've

had some very enthusiastic discussions over the needs of the society in recent months. I believe, though, that things will begin to calm down a bit now." A subtle smile crept across her face. "Here, please take a membership application and turn it in to Sadie out front whenever you're finished. I'll give you a call as soon as the other board members have confirmed your acceptance. Good to see you, Emma. Thank you so much for stopping by."

With that, I was summarily dismissed from Betty's office.

I decided to take the application over to the ice cream shop and indulge in a float while I filled it out. As I walked across the street, I couldn't help but feel like Betty was talking about Preacher Jacob when she mentioned recent disagreements among the historical society board. She seemed almost glad to have him out of the way.

Surely a little lady like that couldn't strangle a man of his size, I thought as I completed the application and sucked down the cool, frozen concoction in my glass.

I looked up as a young mother entered with her daughter, probably kindergarten-aged. I couldn't help but wonder if it might be this very child who made the drawing for Preacher Jacob's memorial.

As I passed the church on my way back to return the application to the historical society, I saw Prudence Huffler out front, fussing with all the candles and mementos. I stopped to check on her.

"Prudence?" I started to walk toward her, but her back was to me and I unwittingly startled her, making her jump.

"Yes!" She spun around with a snippy tone, undoubtedly embarrassed at having been so easily startled.

"Hi, you might not remember me...I'm Emma Hooper." I gave her a sympathetic smile.

"Emma...Hooper, you say?" She paused, then seemed to have a flash of recognition. "Oh, you're Ms. Dorothy and Mr.

Ed's granddaughter, aren't you? Of course. I didn't know you were back in town." She was speaking to me, but her eyes darted all around, and her hand was affixed to her chest near the neckline of her dress.

"Yes, I came back." I remembered the lie I'd told everyone and added, "To spend some time with my Grandparents. Listen, I'm so sorry to hear about Preacher Jacob! I didn't know him well, but he certainly seemed like a good man, and so well-loved by the community."

She pulled a handkerchief out of the cuff of her sweater – a move I'd never seen anyone do in real-life before – and dabbed it to her eyes. Her face was swollen and a little red. She had, no doubt, been crying since his death.

"Thank you, Emma," she replied. "He meant so much...so very much..." She looked down at the array of memorials on the ground, then seemed to remember she was meant to be speaking to me. "Well, to everyone in the town. You know, just the other day, I was telling a dear, special friend that, well, you just don't know what you've got..." Her voice cracked, and the tears started again. "You don't know until it's gone forever. He was definitely one-of-a-kind, and now I'll never see him again!"

I noticed the telling slip, where she had said "I" instead of "we". I tried to comfort her, putting an arm around her shoulder.

"He just, he just..." She was heaving now, each breath labored as her face contorted into a full-blown ugly cry. "He could be so steadfast sometimes. I tried to tell him to take..." She paused and looked at me, as if she had forgotten I was there. "To take care in his decisions. If only he hadn't gone to the fort that night."

She wailed, and buried her face into my shoulder.

I was trying to be kind, patting her back. "There, there," I said. "Just let it out." At the same time, I had a growing

71

concern that a puddle of snot was forming on my tear-drenched shoulder.

She suddenly pulled away and stood up very straight. "I'm sorry. I'm-I'm so sorry. I should go."

She quickly turned and walked into the church.

Okay, even for her that was weird, I thought.

Then I continued down to the historical society to turn in my application.

CHAPTER 10

*B*illy arrived just a few minutes before six o'clock.

I was in the sitting room with Grandma, Grandpa, and Snowball. We were all watching a game show when we heard the tap on the screen door. I hopped up to let him in.

"Hi, Billy!" I said, suddenly a little nervous.

"Hey, Emma! Mr. & Mrs. Hooper, how are you both?" He gave my grandparents a beaming smile.

My grandpa rose at once and shook his hand.

"Mighty fine, Billy, mighty fine. Good to see you here on a social call, isn't it, Dorothy?" He looked at my grandma.

"Certainly is!" She smiled, but her attention quickly returned to the TV.

"You wanna come in and sit a spell with us?" Grandpa asked. He had always liked Billy, even when we were little.

"Thank you, sir, but I think we'd better get going. We want to get some fishing in at Ford's Cross before it gets dark." Billy smiled again. "Another time though, maybe?"

I grabbed my bag and patted Snowball on the head, and followed Billy out the front door.

He opened the passenger side of his truck for me, and I climbed in, thankful for the running boards to give me a boost up. As he hopped in behind the driver's seat, he gave me a smile I knew well.

"Now, Emma, I know you've been gone for a while, so try not to feel bad when I catch more than you, okay?" He winked at me.

"Oh, Billy boy! Don't *you* feel bad when you get out-fished by a girl...and an adopted New Yorker, at that!" We both laughed. The nerves from the front door had subsided a little but were still there.

Come on, Emma! You've known him your whole life. Just because he got taller and cuter doesn't change anything.

I decided to change the subject. "So, do you get to come fish up here often?" I asked.

"Not as often as I'd like. The office keeps me pretty busy. Being the only game in town has its advantages, but it has drawbacks, too, like the long hours. People call me at all hours of the day and night and ask if I'll meet them at the office to see them about this or that." He shrugged.

"Oh! I saw Prudence today, out in front of the church."

"Oh, yeah? How's she holdin' up? Not so good, I bet," he said, looking a little concerned.

"Yeah, not so good is right. She was on the front lawn of the church and kept going on and on about how she had told someone that you don't know what you've got until it's gone. Then she cried on my shoulder. It was bad – I mean, big, ugly-crying," I replied.

Billy let out a half-chuckle. "Well, she is right. Sometimes you don't know what you've got until it's gone, for sure." He raised an eyebrow and gave me a side-glance. "Isn't that why you're here? Trying to recapture something from your past?

"I told you about the accident. I'm just trying to take it

easy and recover." I smiled, hoping he would take the answer at face value.

"Whatever you say. I've known you a long time – maybe longer than anyone outside your family, and I know when you're not giving me the whole story. But it's okay," he said, squeezing my hand. "I know you'll tell me the rest when you're ready." He gave me that smile that let me know he had my back. It comforted me, but at the same time, made me feel guilty for not having stayed in touch with him all this time.

Billy and Suzy had both gone away to college, just like I had. Although we loved our families, and had a great childhood growing up in Hillbilly Hollow, we all wanted to get some experience in the outside world. Suzy had always wanted to be a fashion designer, so I wasn't really surprised to see that she had opened up her own clothing store after returning to our home town. Billy had always wanted to be a doctor, from the time we were little. He couldn't stand to see anyone or anything in pain.

I remembered when we were in maybe the third grade, he'd found a bird on the ground. It had apparently flown into the glass of the Stone's living room window. He couldn't stand the thought of it dying. He brought it in and put it in a little shoebox. He got books from the library, and even called the local farm veterinarian for advice. He fed it mushed up crackers mixed with milk, and nursed it back to health until, a couple of weeks later, it could fly away. That's who he was. He was the guy who took care of others.

I was a little different. I didn't have a specific direction when I left for college. I had always enjoyed art and liked to draw, but it wasn't until I was in school that I realized graphic design could even be a career option. My main focus in going to college was to get out of town and see someplace new. After I graduated, one of my first interviews was with a firm in New York and I had jumped at the chance to move to the city. It was everything I had dreamed about. Sure, it was busy and crowded, and there was a conspicuous lack of green space. Still, I enjoyed my job, my apartment, and my friends.

Being back home, though, I was starting to wonder if I had made the right choice. My friends in New York were fun, but they didn't know me like my friends here. We had grown up together. We had weathered broken bones and broken hearts together. All for one, and one for all.

My wandering thoughts returned to the present, as we pulled alongside the road and parked next to a little footpath that lead over to Ford's Cross. The small lake was on a piece of property that was owned by the Ford family in the nineteenth century.

According to folklore, the Fords were part of the Underground Railroad, and anyone who could cross the narrow, shallow part of the lake and make it to the barn at the back of the homestead would receive help. The Fords had family in Cairo, which bordered the free state of Illinois, and would give food, shelter, and directions to those who needed their help. Thus the small lake came to be known as Ford's Cross. That was one thing that was interesting about Hillbilly Hollow– everywhere you turned there was history.

Billy grabbed the poles and bait from the back of the truck, and handed me a small, soft-sided cooler.

"What's in here?" I asked, holding up the cooler as I followed him down the path.

"You'll see." He laughed and picked up the pace. "Hurry up, Emma. We're burnin' daylight."

We found the spot where some rocks and an old felled tree jutted out over the water, and started fishing.

We spent the next couple of hours fishing. We talked some, but mostly just enjoyed being outside on a beautiful afternoon. Billy caught a blue catfish and a couple of small-mouth Bass. I didn't manage to catch anything other than an empty pop bottle.

Billy pulled together a few twigs and branches to make a small fire, and used the fire steel on his keychain to start it.

"Dinner?" he asked, holding up the cooler.

"Sure!"

He found a large, flat-ish rock and set it in the middle of the fire, then took a packet of foil from the cooler and set it on the rock. Within about fifteen minutes, we were eating fried chicken, along with some potato salad from a couple of plastic containers.

"So, did I tell you I joined the historical society?" I asked.

"No! Wow. If your New York friends could see you in a prairie dress and bonnet!" He laughed. "So does that mean you're sticking around for a while?" His eyes were a mixture of surprise and hopefulness.

"Well, ya know, you guys missed me an awful lot, so I thought I'd better." I laughed. "Although, it's sure not the hometown I thought I was coming back to with a murderer on the loose. Tucker came by Suzy's shop while I was there and put up a flyer – like the one I saw in your clinic window. Anyway, he didn't seem to have much of a clue where to start."

Billy finished chewing his bite of chicken and took a chug from one of the bottled waters he had brought.

"Come on, Emma. When has Tuck ever had much of a clue about anything other than running a football down the field, or catching an outfield fly?"

"Hmm, jealous of the star athlete much?" I raised an eyebrow at him playfully.

"That dufus? Heck, no! I'll take my brain over his brawn any day." He smiled smugly.

"Well, you're not that skinny kid anymore yourself, Billy.

You've got plenty of brawn to go with that big ol' brain of yours." I smiled coyly.

He laughed and shook his head. "Well, all I know is if we're waiting for Tucker to figure out who the killer is, we'll be waiting until we're old and gray. I don't know. It's kind of hard to imagine anyone we know being capable of that. Do you suppose it could've been a stranger? Someone passing through?"

"I guess, but to what end? Why would a stranger randomly stop by the old fort looking for...what? Someone to rob? Or someone to murder? No, I don't think so. You said he was strangled with a haversack strap. He wasn't shot – shooting is impersonal. To strangle someone, I mean..."

Billy wore an unbuttoned long-sleeved shirt over his t-shirt. I reached up and grabbed both sides of the collar and held them together. "I mean, look how close you'd have to be to kill someone that way."

"You've been watching too many cop shows." He chuckled. "You're right – it does seem personal, but you've got it wrong. Here, I'll show you. Turn around."

I turned my back to him, and he took a dishtowel from the cooler, and twisted it into a rope-like shape.

"It was like this," he said. He took one end of the towel in each hand, and carefully looped it over my head, then pulled the ends together at the back of my neck and pulled down.

"Leverage – like this, see?" He tugged on it gently.

A shiver ran down my spine. For a brief second, I had a glimpse of what it must have been like to be Preacher Jacob in his final moments.

"You okay?" Billy asked, releasing one end of the towel, and putting a hand on my shoulder. "I didn't hurt you, did I?"

"Oh, no, of course not. Just...what's that saying? Someone walking over my grave?"

We sat there a little while longer, until the lightning bugs were dancing in the evening sky. Then we doused the camp-fire, and piled everything back into the truck, including Billy's fish and my pop bottle for the recycling bin.

Then we drove back to my grandparents' farm.

Billy hopped out of the truck and walked me to the front door.

"Listen, I know you're just as interested as everyone else in finding out what happened to Preacher Jacob, but... whoever did this surely doesn't wanna be found out, and I don't want anything to happen to you. Just promise me you'll be careful?"

"I promise. Don't worry – unless they're driving a taxi, I think I'll be alright." I pointed to the side of my scalp and shrugged. "Thanks for tonight. It was fun."

"I had fun too." He put his arms out, and I put mine around his neck to give him a hug. "This is a much better way for you to have your hands around my neck." He laughed, and squeezed me tightly.

"Billy Stone, are you tryin' to flirt with me?" I asked play-fully as we stepped apart.

"Not many single girls in town, ya know. It's pretty much you or Prudence Huffler, and you're just *that* much cuter!" He pinched his thumb and forefinger together and winked as he turned to walk back to his truck.

"Whatever, Billy! If you're gonna be like that I'll start flirting with Larry Tucker! I hear he's single!"

"Yeah, good luck with that!" he said sarcastically, throwing his hand up in the air as he opened his door. "Night, Emma!"

"Night, Billy." I waved and went inside.

* * *

I GOT a glass of water from the tap in the kitchen, and as I stood at the sink, I couldn't help but picture Preacher Jacob's final moments. Billy had tugged down on the towel when he showed me what had happened. That had to mean the murderer was shorter than the victim.

I pulled out my phone and took a look at the memorial page on the historical society website again. I scrolled through several photos of Preacher Jacob with different townspeople. There were several in which Prudence was in the background, just a few feet away, at old fort days and a couple with Betty and other members of the historical society. I then came across one with Preacher Jacob in his cavalry officer's uniform, standing next to Tucker in his sheriff's uniform. Tucker was about six feet tall or maybe six-one, and in that photo, Preacher Jacob looked a little taller. Billy had indicated the strangulation came from behind and below.

Does that really mean the murderer had to be shorter than the victim or could there be some other reason for the angle?

I decided I should get ready for bed now that I was on country time, and brushed my teeth at the kitchen sink. I headed out back to the outhouse before I turned in for the night, with my furry little shadow, Snowball, in tow.

As we got about twenty-five feet from the outhouse itself, Snowball let out a short bleat, and lay down in the middle of the path as she had a couple of nights before.

I looked up ahead into the darkness at the edge of the woods behind the outhouse and couldn't see anything out of the usual. I looked back at her.

"Snowball? What's wrong?"

She stuck her tongue out at me. She was a pugnacious little goat.

I continued on toward the outhouse and, still seeing nothing unusual, I went inside and took care of business. Afterward, I walked out of the structure, closed the little wooden door, and crossed the yard to the back of the farmhouse.

As I glanced back the way I had just come, something out of the corner of my vision caught my attention.

I saw the same figure I had seen before, this time near the outhouse I had just left. The figure was bent over, as if it was fussing with something on the ground. Suddenly, its arms went up as if it was clutching at its throat. It thrashed back and forth, then fell to the ground. I took a step forward, and the figure rose, pointing emphatically toward the old fort.

I steeled my nerves and stepped even closer. I looked around to see if Grandpa or anyone else was outside, but it was just Snowball and me.

I cleared my throat, realizing that what I was about to do was either brave or crazy.

"Are you Preacher Jacob?" I asked softly.

The figure didn't respond, but instead went through the entire pantomime again. Bent over, doing something on the floor, clutching at its throat, and falling over. Once again, it arose and pointed toward the fort emphatically.

"Do you – do you want me to go see something at the fort?" I asked.

It made a jerky movement that was more nodding its whole body forward than nodding its head and again pointed toward the fort.

"Okay, I think I understand." I looked over my shoulder again. "I'll try to help – I'll do my best. But then you have to leave me alone. Do we have a deal?" As I said the last word, the ghost disappeared.

I'm not fluent in ghost speak, but I think that was an agreement.

I walked back down the path toward the house, and as I passed Snowball, she hopped up to join me.

"Well, Snowball, I don't know about you, but I'm starting

to have my doubts about this whole idea of these visions just being electrical impulses in my brain. Whadya reckon?"

She didn't make a sound, but as I opened the back kitchen door, she rubbed up against my legs like a cat, then swatted at my leg with one small hoof.

I picked her up and took her up to the attic, where we turned in for the night.

CHAPTER 11

*I*n the wee hours of the morning, a strange sound stirred me from my sleep.

The noise reminded me of the first apartment I'd had in New York, a place that had backed up to a row of restaurants and businesses. Neighborhood cats would gather near the dumpsters, looking for treats or rodents to catch. They would often sit atop the dumpsters and yowl to each other. The noise was, at least in my tired mind, something like that. Almost like a yowl, with a sound in the background that was almost like a person talking or singing. The sound was followed shortly after by the scrape of metal on metal.

One of the animals must've knocked over a bucket. That or one of the gutters is loose. I'll have Grandpa check it tomorrow, I thought groggily as I drifted back off to sleep.

* * *

LATER IN THE MORNING, I was helping Grandpa bale hay, when my phone buzzed in my pocket.

"Hello?" I answered.

"Hello, Ms. Hooper? This is Kara calling from National Airlines. I have some great news about your bag," the voice on the other end said cheerily.

"Finally! Is it being delivered?" I asked.

"Unfortunately," she began and I cut her off.

"Please don't. Don't say unfortunately again. Where is it now? Miami? Portland? Timbuktu?" I asked, incredulous that I could still be without my luggage.

"Oh no, ma'am! It's in Branson! Unfortunately, our delivery driver has a bad case of food poisoning, so he can't bring it to you. If you'd like to come get it, though…"

I cut her off, but this time, with enthusiasm instead of frustration. "Yes! I'll come get it right away. Just tell me where I should go." I put the phone on speaker, much to Grandpa's dismay, and used the notes app to record the instructions. After I hung up, I excitedly told him, "They've found my bag and I need to go to Branson to get it."

"You go on ahead, then. I know you've been waitin' a while for that thing to show up. I'll finish up here," Grandpa replied.

"Thanks, Grandpa!" I said enthusiastically before running into the house to change.

After I got cleaned up, I made the hour-long drive down to Branson. I arrived at the airport, and found the lost luggage office at the back of the space by the baggage carousels where I had initially looked for my bag when I landed a few nights before.

There was a couple standing in the tiny lost baggage office of National Airlines with four children in tow, two of whom were screaming their lungs out. I decided to stand near the carousel and wait for them to clear out.

As I was standing against the wall, a gaggle of passengers approached the luggage carousel near me, apparently from a flight that has just landed. One of them was a huge man with long, black hair and a long beard to match. He was tan and clearly looked a bit too old for ebony to be his natural hair color. His voice boomed as he spoke to the man next to him. Both of them wore jeans, button-down shirts, sport coats, and cowboy boots. The larger man had on sunglasses, and a straw cowboy hat with a huge spray of feathers at the front. As he was speaking, I finally recognized him as the lead singer of Ozark Mountain Lightning, a five-man country band that was popular in the 90s. They were famous for their melodic harmonies, and they had a huge crossover hit with the upbeat song, *Hello Suzy Q*. It was the same song we used to torture Suzy with when we were young.

As I looked around at the airport signs, it occurred to me that a lot of the big country acts from decades past had set up residences in Branson. It was, after all, the Vegas of the Ozarks. Seeing that the family was still animatedly talking to the National Airlines rep in the office, I thought I'd distract myself with a little B-list celebrity eavesdropping. I stepped closer to get a better angle from which to hear.

"So anyway, Danny, and let me tell ya, this man was serious, I mean serious as a heart attack," the singer, whose name I couldn't remember at the time, said to his friend. "And he looks me right in the eye and says, 'I swear it on my Mama's grave, that's the truth.' I mean, can you believe that?"

"So Don," the other man began to speak.

Don Clark! That's him, I remembered.

"Now, Don, I just don't know if I believe in all that! You're telling me this fella got hit in the head with a softball at his daughter's game, and after that, he started seeing ghosts?" As the man shook his head, continuing the conversation, my stomach wrenched into a knot. I stepped back a little, leaning against the wall.

What if this is...really a thing? Maybe that accident really did trigger something in my brain after all, I thought. *Maybe I should talk to Billy about it? He knows me – he knows I'm normally a stable person.*

I saw the family with the stair-stepped children finally leave the baggage office, so I went in to claim my bag. I was beyond relieved to see my giant purple suitcase sitting in the back room.

After showing my ID and signing a form, I received my bag and headed back to the farm.

The man's words from the airport kept ringing in my ears. *Hit in the head...started seeing ghosts.* I knew I had to see if I could get online and do some research on this when I got back.

As I got off the highway that connected Elmore, where the interstate exit was, to Hillbilly Hollow, my phone buzzed. I pulled into a gas station to answer it.

"Hello, Emma! This is Betty Blackwood. I have some very good news for you! The other board members have agreed to accept your membership into the historical society!" She said it with a lilt in her voice as if I'd just won a major award.

"Oh, that *is* great news, thank you so much," I replied, knowing I'd done so less enthusiastically than she wanted me to.

"Well, if you could come by this afternoon, you can pick up your orientation package. There's a lot about the fort's history, and the town's, that you'll need to know so you can get started."

"Oh, of course. I'll be in town anyway for the vigil," I replied.

"Mm, of course. How *could* I forget? We'll see you soon then, Emma. Welcome to the society!" She hung up the phone abruptly.

My luggage was in the back of the crew cab of the truck and it was getting late, so I decided to head on into town and grab a bite to eat at the Hollow Diner after I picked up my paperwork. The truck I was driving was the old farm truck. Grandpa still had the *new* farm truck and Grandma's car at the house so they'd drive down for the vigil on their own.

I stopped by the historical society and saw Betty for my paperwork. I was surprised to learn that there was an actual swearing in that went along with the signed document and pin.

Serious business, indeed.

Betty told me I could go to the fort the following day and see Richard Littman, and he would give me the tour and go over some of the points of interest.

I knew Mr. Littman. He was maybe a few years younger than my grandparents. He used to own the bookstore in town, but he retired when I was in high school and sold it to the Chapmans, who bulldozed it and put up a gas station in its place. Mr. Littman's house was not too far from Billy's place in town, and I remembered that when I was a little girl he gave out the best Halloween candy. Mostly, though, I liked him because whenever he saw me, he didn't give me a look of pity about losing my parents. Instead, he would tell me funny or silly stories about when they were young. People didn't know how to treat a child whose whole world had just imploded, but Mr. Littman was more intuitive than most people. I couldn't wait to see him.

I headed to the Hollow Diner to grab a bite, and texted Suzy and Billy in case either of them wanted to join me before the vigil.

I sat down and immediately recognized the waitress who came to take my order as Sherrie Selby. She was in our class in school, and we never got along. She always teased me about my grandparents' house not being big or fancy like hers. The summer after our senior year, though, her father ran off with a backup singer from one of the shows down in Branson, and her and her mom had to sell the house and move into a trailer on a small piece of property at the outskirts of town.

Sherrie was still pretty and blonde, but the years had not been kind. She definitely had a hard edge about her, and looked much older than thirty.

"Emma Hooper! What in the world are you doin' in town?" she asked, slapping a laminated menu down with a *thwap!*

"Hi, Sherrie. I'm in town visiting my grandparents for a while. How are you?" I asked politely.

"I'm real good, thanks. How 'bout you?" Sherrie smiled but I could tell she wasn't especially fond of the idea of welcoming me home.

"Oh, just great, thanks. Could I get a root beer please?" I smiled up at her.

"Well, if it isn't my favorite doctor." Her tone suddenly got soft and syrupy sweet.

I didn't have to turn around. I knew it was Billy walking up behind me.

"Sherrie," he said with a brief nod, then plopped down in the booth next to me, resting his arm on the back of my chair. "Hi, Emma," he said squeezing me as he whispered into my ear, "Play along."

"What kept you so long?" I replied, leaning next to him. "I didn't know how long it would take you to finish up at the clinic, so I didn't order you a drink yet. What can Sherrie bring you?" I fluttered my eyelashes at him and we both tried not to crack up.

"Coffee would be great, thanks, Sherrie," he said and quickly turned back to me.

I backhanded him in the stomach as she walked off and he put his arm down.

"What are you doing?" I asked, looking up at him from under my brows.

"She's always tryin' to get me to ask her out. She swears I keep dodging her because I've been holding a torch for you since high school." He shook his head.

"You've been what? I'm sorry?" I asked, incredulously.

"It's not – I – she's exaggerating," he said nervously, then mumbled something I couldn't hear under his breath.

"Sorry, come again? Didn't quite catch that," I said, raising an eyebrow at him and enjoying watching him squirm.

"It's nothing. I said…I said it's not a torch. A match, maybe." Even through his tanned skin, I knew his face well enough to see when he was blushing. We both laughed.

"Well, a fireplace match at least, I would hope." I changed the subject. "Have you heard from Suzy?"

"Yeah, she and Brian are going to meet us here in just a bit. Thought we'd grab a bite then head over to the church. Are your grandparents comin'?" he asked.

"Yeah, I'm sure they'll be here. Oh! I almost forgot." I pulled the pin out of my bag to show him. "Guess who's an *official* member of the historical society now?"

"Hey, congrats! You won Mrs. Blackwood over, I see." He smiled.

"Yes. *Just*. While we were talking she went off on some tirade about how much it costs to maintain the fort, and how people don't think about how serious it all is. It was like she was off in her own world. It was really strange."

"What's strange?" Suzy asked as she walked in with Brian.

"Brian! So good to see you! I'd get up to hug you, but I'm pinned, as you see," I said, pointing to Billy who was on the outside of the booth.

"Great to see you too, Emma. Suzy's been on and on about you being back since you got here." Brian smiled at Suzy with a look that was pure love. She was right, he really did seem like a good guy these days.

"Yeah, yeah, everybody is glad Emma's back." I felt Suzy kick my shin under the table.

"Ow! What was that for?" I looked at her, wide-eyed, as I rubbed my shin.

"Oh, sorry! Short legs. That wasn't meant for you." She gave Billy a stern look, then returned to me. "*As I said*, what's strange?"

Sherrie returned and set down my root beer and Billy's coffee. "Hey Sherrie," Suzy said, "He'll have a pop," she crooked a thumb at Brian, "and I'll have a diet because I have a dress to fit into soon. And, could we get menus too please? Thanks!" She quickly returned her gaze to me, waiting for a response.

"Oh, well, when Mrs. Blackwood was interviewing me for the historical society, she went off on some tangent about money, and people not understanding how important the fort was…really strange."

"Tell 'em." Suzy slapped Brian in the chest with the back of her hand. "Tell 'em what you told me, go on."

Same ol' Suzy – still bossy!

"Oh, well, I was picking up a chandelier for my mom at Teller's last week." He looked around and leaned in as if he thought a secret could be kept long in a town this size. "Anyhow, I see Mayor Teller talking to Preacher Jacob over in his office. The office door was cracked open, so you could hear 'em a little. Anyway, they were arguing, and Preacher Jacob kept shakin' his head back and forth and Mayor Teller was making that chopping motion with his hand, like he was tryin' to make a point." Brian demonstrated.

He continued with, "The only thing I heard him say clearly was when Teller raised his voice real loud. Man, his face was red." Brian shook his head at the memory. "Anyway, he said, 'I need to see it! I'll pay any price,' then something like, 'I don't care – bring it to me'. Just then, the shop clerk,

Lena, she walked out from the back with the chandelier, and as she walked by Teller's office she shut the door. So that was all I could hear. Crazy, really. After that, I saw him at church on Sunday, then he was just gone. I couldn't believe it."

"Wow, that sounds like it was quite an exchange," I said. "Did you tell Tucker?"

"I did, but he didn't seem to think there was much to it," Brian replied.

Suzy looked at me, and she and I mouthed the same words at the same time: *box of rocks.* We both started laughing hysterically.

"Any ideas what they're laughing at?" Brian asked Billy.

"No clue, man, no clue," he replied.

"Oh, Suzy, I nearly forgot! When I picked up my suitcase, I saw Don Clark at the airport. You know, from Ozark Mountain Lightning?"

Billy looked at me and we both immediately started singing *Hello Suzy Q.*

Suzy rolled her eyes. "You're both gonna get it, just so you know!" She picked up one of Brian's fries and threw it at me. "And *you* started it!"

After chatting for a while, we all headed over to the vigil.

CHAPTER 12

*W*hen we got to the church, all the older folks, including my grandparents, had lawn chairs on the sidewalk and crowds of people were already in the street. Tucker and his deputies had the street blocked off to through traffic, their white headlights flashing onto the storefronts across from the church.

Suzy, Brian, Billy, and I stood behind my grandparents, and Suzy's grandmother, who was sitting beside them. Danny Baxter, the Youth Pastor, stepped up and said a few words while some of the teenagers from the congregation passed out candles stuck through little paper plates to everyone gathered.

Next to Danny stood Betty Blackwood, who followed him, walking to the top step of the church door to reiterate the reward the historical society was offering. She may have just been historical society president, but she should've gone into government politics the way she worked that crowd. I couldn't help but feel she didn't miss Preacher Jacob quite as much as she would like to have people think.

I half-expected Prudence to get up and say something

about Preacher Jacob, but she was an absolute wreck. Her mother, Margene, was doing her best to hold her up as she sobbed and wailed. Eventually, she got some help from a couple of the older church deacons. One of the old men from the sidewalk stood up and waved them all over to where he was, offering Prudence his aluminum, green-and-white webbed chair. She collapsed into it as if she had lost all will to go on.

At the end of the vigil, Tucker stood up and reminded everyone again that they wanted to speak to anyone who saw Preacher Jacob on the day of his death, or who had any information on anything unusual in the area near the old fort that night.

As he spoke, Suzy and I both leaned forward, around Brian and each put a hand up to shield our lips from onlookers as we simultaneously mouthed the words, 'crazy handsome.' We suppressed an inappropriate giggle as we each covered our mouths with our hands and stood back upright.

As people started to scatter, Grandma said she'd like to go by Margene Huffler's place and help her see to Prudence.

"Emma, that means you need to ride back with me," Grandpa said.

"Oh, Mr. Hooper, I'll make sure she gets home," Suzy said putting a hand on his arm sweetly.

"Oh, okay," I replied, handing Grandpa the keys to the old truck. "My suitcase is in the back, so could you leave the truck unlocked when you get home please?" I leaned forward and gave him a peck on the cheek.

"Always do. Be careful, kids," he said to all of us and none of us in particular before he picked up the folding chairs and walked down the block toward the truck.

I walked with Suzy, Brian and Billy back toward the end of the business district.

"Well, we're over here," Suzy said. "Talk to you tomorrow, Emma. Goodnight, you guys." She grabbed Brian's hand and turned down the side street.

"Wait a minute, you're supposed to take me home," I protested.

"No, I said I'd *make sure* you get home. Billy, take her home. 'Night!"

She laughed and walked off with Brian, who just shrugged apologetically.

Billy and I turned to look at each other, and said in unison, "She's *so* bossy!"

We laughed, and I told him, "I'm sorry. If I'd known you'd get saddled with driving me, I would've gone with Grandpa."

"I don't mind. The truck's at my house. Hey – since we have to go by, you can pop in and see my place!" His smile was beaming and I couldn't say no.

"Sounds great. Let's go!"

We walked the two blocks further to Billy's, and he let me in the front door.

I was in awe when I saw the inside. There was no telling how much he had spent remodeling the place.

"You did *all of this*?" I asked as I waved my hand around in the air.

"Pretty much. I did have some help for the big stuff, though. Like putting in the ceramic tile in the kitchen, and the plumbing – not willing to take a DIY risk with that. I refinished the floors though...installed all those light fixtures." He pointed to some beautiful antique-style light fixtures above us. "Come on, I'll show you my favorite room."

He took me through the open living room to a wall of glass at the back of the house, and slid open the back door. We stepped out into the back yard. There was a huge deck with an outdoor kitchen and a fire pit surrounded by big, soft lounge chairs.

"Wow! You made fun of me for watching detective shows, but you must watch home improvement TV nonstop. This is amazing!"

I couldn't remember having been in a home that was any nicer than his was. As we walked through it, I had remembered the dark, burgundy wallpaper and hunter green carpet that had been inside before. The modern, hardwood floors, big windows, and light colors were a nice contrast and a huge improvement overall.

"Have a seat – I'll grab you a pop. We can chat a bit before we head out." He hopped up the two steps onto the deck, then quickly turned back. "I mean, if that's okay with you?"

I nodded, and he smiled, going back inside to retrieve two bottles of pop. I decided to make myself at home on the comfortable chair.

I lounged back on the chair, thinking how relaxing it must be to sit out here and read, or just look up at the stars.

Suddenly, something furry leapt up onto the chair next to me, and I jumped. The chair lost its balance, and I fell back, feet over head, and found myself face down on the lawn next to the upturned chair.

I heard a *yip,* and before I know it, the little fur ball was standing directly in front of me, and we were eye-to-eye as I lifted myself up on my elbows. It immediately licked my face, yipping again, and wagging its tail.

"You could warn a girl before you pounce, you know!" I said to the cute little furry face.

"What?" Billy asked, coming back outside. "Oh no! Emma! Are you okay?"

He put the pop down on the edge of the fire pit and grabbed me underneath the arms, pulling me to my feet.

"There you go. You're okay, I think. Nothing hurts?" he asked, looking carefully at my eyes in doctor-patient examination mode.

"I think it's broken," I replied, rubbing my hand across my chest just under my neck.

"What's broken? Show me! Where?" He urgently began scanning my neck and collarbone.

"My pride. It's toast!" I smiled at him.

"Emma." He raised an eyebrow at me. "That's not funny to do to a doctor, ya know."

"Right, right. Dr. Billy. I keep forgetting. Sorry!" I smiled.

He turned the chair back right side up and I sat down, more cautiously.

The pup put its paws up on the edge of the chair, and I picked her up this time, making sure she didn't startle me again. Billy sat on the foot of the chair next to me, and I couldn't help but think he wanted to weigh the chair down to make sure I didn't flip it again.

"She's so cute! What kind is she?" I asked.

The pup immediately curled up on my lap, her little tail wagging a mile a minute.

"She's, well, she's a Maltipoo. Her name is Halee," he said sheepishly.

"A Maltipoo? Didn't you have Labradors and Coon Hounds growing up? Big tough guy grows up and gets this sweet little baby?" I gave a full belly laugh.

"What can I say? One of my patients had to give her up. When I saw that fluffy hair, and those big, dark eyes, I couldn't resist." He reached over and patted her on the head.

She seemed to be pretty happy to be getting petted by two people at one time. I could just imagine her putting those little paws up on Billy's leg, and him looking down into those big puppy eyes and giving her whatever she wanted.

"Mm-hm. So *this* is the lady in your life? Does Sherrie Selby know? She'll be crushed!" I laughed again and he threw me a feigned look of being wounded.

"If you're just gonna insult me all night..." he started.

"No, I'm just kidding. I'm kind of glad you asked me to come over for a bit before we headed back. There's something I've been wanting to talk to you about, but I wasn't sure how to say it, exactly."

He leaned forward a bit in anticipation.

I nervously looked down, stroking Halee's head between her ears.

"It's about the accident. I told you about getting hit, in New York. I didn't tell you the whole story." I went on to tell him how I'd heard the singer and his friend talk about seeing ghosts after a head injury when I was at the airport, and how I'd had a similar experience. "So, what do you think? Have you ever heard of it? Is it something…I'll *ever* get past?"

"Hang tight, I'll be right back." He disappeared into the house and came out a moment later with a tablet. "I've got some professional references downloaded on here. Let me see what I can find."

He scanned the device for a couple of minutes. "Okay, here we go! You're – I'm asking from a purely medical standpoint here – you're not on any medications are you?"

"Oh, no. I was on an anti-inflammatory when I first got out of the hospital, but nothing now," I replied.

"Okay, that's good…" he continued reading. "And do you remember the doctor saying it was a diffuse injury or focal?"

"Diffuse sounds familiar. Please tell me that's a good sign," I said.

"It could be. Emma, it sounds like you had a pretty serious injury. If it was diffuse…" He moved his hand back and forth all over his scalp area to demonstrate. "…that means it was more widespread, but that type of injury is associated with hallucinations like you describe, especially when they begin soon after the injury. When was the onset?"

I was floored by how proper and official he sounded

talking about medical stuff. I knew he was a doctor, of course, but he was also little Billy Stone.

I said, "Um, the onset, like when it started? As soon as I got out of the hospital. Three days, maybe?"

"Okay, well, that could be a good sign. As the axons heal, those are the nerve cells that carry cerebral activity, they'll rewire themselves and you should start feeling back to normal. It could take weeks, or months maybe, but it should happen."

He put the tablet down on the empty chair next to us and patted Halee, who was comfortably draped across my lap, on the head.

"Thanks. That does make me feel a bit better. It's just uncanny, though, that I saw that…that…whatever it is in the field the same night Preacher Jacob was murdered. I don't understand it." I sighed.

"Probably just coincidence – or projection. You heard from Tucker about Preacher Jacob the next morning, and you made that blob become him because it fit. Your brain was just trying to make sense of something nonsensical," he replied.

Darn he was cute when he was being all smart and logical.

"Billy?" I asked.

"Yes, Emma?"

"When did you get so smart?"

We both laughed.

"I feel like I should say college," he answered. "I'm not going to be smart tomorrow if I don't get some sleep, though. Ready to head back up to the farm?"

I nodded my head, and gently picked up Halee and deposited her on the chair.

He took my hand and helped me up.

"Steady there, Emma." He chuckled.

I put my arms up around his neck and pulled him down to hug me.

"Thanks, Billy," I whispered in his ear.

"Anything for a fellow musketeer," he replied, squeezing me tightly.

CHAPTER 13

*W*hen I got home, Grandpa had put my suitcase up in the attic for me, but he was already in bed.

It felt completely shallow to think it, but I was thrilled to have my own face cleanser, a few more pairs of underwear, and shoes that weren't either boots or flip-flops to wear.

The old truck was back, so I assumed Grandma was in bed as well.

Snowball was not pleased to smell Billy's pup on my clothes, and bleated at me, then came and nudged me as I lay down in the bed, hoping for some scratches under the chin.

"You're a good girl, Snowball. I did pet a dog, that's true, but nothing comes between a girl and her goat," I told her.

Despite the somber tone of the vigil, I felt surprisingly relaxed. I got to sleep in what seemed like no time. Once again, though, the noise from those cats, or whatever it was, woke me up at about four-thirty in the morning. I tried to wake up a little more, determined to figure out where it was coming from this time.

I stuck my head out the round window of the attic, and

was sure the sound was coming from the roof above me. I listened intently, and could've sworn it was a tune.

I put on my muck boots and headed downstairs and out the kitchen door, where I heard the distinct thud of metal on metal. I looked to the end of the back porch, and there was Grandpa with the straight ladder, starting to climb up to the top of the roof.

"Grandpa," I said, "Did they wake you too?"

"Emma! What? Did who wake me?" he asked gruffly.

"The cats! Isn't that a cat wailing on the roof? How'd it get up there?" I asked.

"It's no cat," he said, looking toward the roof. "Just a minute, let me take care of this."

He ascended the ladder and I heard him walk across the roof of the porch. A moment later I heard a woman's voice, saying, 'What? No, no, no!' Then, he was descending the ladder with my tiny Grandma thrown over his shoulder.

"Grandma?" I asked.

He got to the ground and put her down.

"Are you okay?" I asked her.

"It's Mamie's fault – Mamie's *fault!*" Grandma said, emphasizing her point with a bony finger in the air. "She and Dolly don't get along. Never mind Nancy's the one stirring the pot! Hmpf!"

"What are you…" I started to ask her what was wrong and Grandpa cut me off.

"She can't hear ya, child. She won't remember any of this in the mornin' neither," he said as he took her by the shoulders and guided her to the back door.

I opened the back porch door, and stood in the sitting room as he guided her to the bed. He came back out and sat on the sofa.

"It's just one of her funny spells," Grandpa said. "Nothin' to worry about." He sat back calmly.

"Nothing to worry about? She was on the *roof!* She's seventy, for Heaven's sake!" I was shocked at his nonchalance.

"That she is, but she can still outwork and outrun most people. Child, it's nothin'. She gets this way sometimes. Been goin' on for years. She starts singing at – I don't know! The moon? The chickens? Who knows?" He shook his head. "She won't remember a thing by the mornin'."

"Wait, the…the chickens? Oh, right! Mamie Eisenhower, Dolly Madison…" I replied.

"Don't forget Nancy Reagan. She can't stand that hen!" He let a small chuckle escape, the first one I've heard in years, and patted me on the knee. "Get some sleep, now. I promise I'll look after her. Always have, always will." He smiled and stood, then turned back to me.

"Besides, this is the last one for a while," he added. "This was night number four. Funny spells never go on longer than four nights. 'Night, Emma!"

He walked into the bedroom and shut the door. It really touched me to see how deeply he loved and cared for her.

Okay, I thought. *So, I see dead people, and my Grandma climbs the roof and sings to chickens – chickens she names after first ladies of the United States. That's not troubling at all.*

I headed back up to bed and must have been exhausted because I was back asleep within minutes.

* * *

THE NEXT MORNING, I came downstairs to smell bacon and fresh coffee brewing. "Good morning, Emma, dear!" my grandmother said in a sing-song voice.

"You seem in a good mood this morning, Grandma," I replied. "You must've slept well."

Grandpa was sitting at the table, reading a newspaper. It

was late – almost seven-thirty – since I slept in, so he must've been in for a break after early morning chores. He pulled the corner of the newspaper down and gave me a look over it that told me not to poke at the subject.

"Oh, yes! I slept like a newborn babe! Would you like some breakfast, dear?" she asked.

"Sure, I would," I replied. "Let me just use the bathroom first."

I walked out to the outhouse, not worried about seeing my unwanted visitor since I'd only seen him in the late night hours on the previous nights. Snowball was following me, as usual, and didn't stop in the path, which I took as another good sign. She plopped down in some grass near the outhouse, and I went in and took care of business. When I came out, I called her, and she wouldn't come.

"Snowball, come on, girl. I'll sneak you a bite of biscuit under the table. Come on!"

Still, she wouldn't budge. I had my doubts about getting a stubborn goat to move but decided to give it a try. I walked over to pick her up and almost fell over at the sight of what was next to her.

There, on the ground, was a collection of sticks arranged very clearly to spell the word, *US*.

"Come here, Snowball," I said again."

She bleated at me, seeming annoyed, but didn't look at all frightened.

I determined, based on her behavior the previous nights, that this could only mean the sticks were in place before she lay down. I rubbed my eyes, and looked again, just to be sure. It was as clear as could be. *U-S.* I had my phone in my pocket, so I withdrew it and quickly snapped a photo. Looking around, I made sure no one, and nothing, was watching us. I picked up Snowball and went back into the house.

What's the meaning of the sign? U-S as in us?

The old fort was a Union fort, which meant it was a U.S. fort. I wondered what else it could possibly mean, and knew I would have to think about what, if anything, it was trying to tell me. The alternate theory was some sort of crazy scenario where Snowball was going to start leaving me messages spelled out in twigs. Although nearly as implausible, I thought the idea of Preacher Jacob, or his ghost at least, being behind the message was far more likely.

Back inside, Grandma had a plate ready for me. I went to sit at the table, and a chicken flew up from the chair as I pulled it back.

"Shoo, chicken!" I said as I tipped the chair up to make sure there were no feathers on it before I took a seat.

I quickly ate my breakfast and was excited to get over to the old fort and see Mr. Littman.

I wasn't sure how exactly I was supposed to be dressed, so I put on one of the flowery dresses with short sleeves I had bought from Suzy's place and a pair of comfortable, slip-on shoes from my suitcase. It felt good to have all my regular things back.

CHAPTER 14

I pulled up to the visitor center at Fort Harris and hopped out of the truck.

The visitor center building was not original. The original building, comprised of the quarters of the fort commander and other officers in the company, burned down due to an electrical fire in the early nineteen-forties. The current structure was a faithful recreation that was completed in the early seventies. It was universally regarded by the townspeople as a tragedy that the original building had burned. However, it gave the old fort the advantage of housing a beautiful visitor center with air conditioning, modern bathrooms, and a profitable gift shop.

When I walked into the visitor center building at nine-thirty, Mr. Littman was waiting for me.

"Emma!"

He rushed over and took both my hands in his, kissing me gingerly on the cheek. He was only about five-nine and had always carried a few extra pounds around the middle. Full, rosy cheeks protruded from above his neat salt and pepper beard.

"I'd heard you were in town and had been hoping you'd find time to come and see me, and here you are!" His smile stretched from ear to ear.

"Hi, Mr. Littman! I'm so happy to see you!" I grinned broadly. "How have you been doing?" I asked.

"Oh, very well, I've been wonderful, thanks. And may I say you are even prettier than I remember, though I don't know how that's possible." He winked at me in that very sweet and grandfatherly way of his. "How about you? Decided to shrug off New York to come back home to our sleepy little burg, did you?" He chuckled, and when he did, his whole body shook.

"Something like that," I smiled, not wanting to get into a long discussion about my reasons for coming back. "So, Mrs. Blackwood tells me that you're going to show me the ropes around here. Should we get started?"

Mr. Littman gave me a tour of the visitor center first.

The gift shop was in the center of the building, and you had to pass through it from both the front and back entrances to access either of the public restrooms. It was apparently a strong driver of revenue for the fort and the society. He showed me into the small set of offices at the back of the visitor center that was reserved for members of the historical society. The men's and women's bathrooms, he explained, had doors at the back that opened into small locker rooms that we could use during Old Fort Days, though most residents just arrived in costume. Across the hall was a small break room for the staff of the Visitor Center and grounds.

Mr. Littman handed me a clipboard, a map, and a pen, and we headed out to walk the grounds. He showed me the officers' barracks building and pointed out a dent in the floor. Apparently, a wayward cannonball had come through the barracks window during a drill, destroying a bunk from which Fort Commander Philip Stapleton had just risen.

"Stapleton, you see, didn't want separate quarters. He wanted to be here, with his men, in the trenches, as it were," Mr. Littman explained.

The cannonball was housed on a stand in the corner of the room. I made some notes on the interesting story. I walked to the back where a smaller gun rack as well as one for swords, stood along the wall. Mr. Littman confirmed that this was where the officers kept their weapons while they slept.

As I walked along the weapons racks, I felt a chill run down my spine at the back corner of the room.

"Is this building temperature controlled?" I asked.

"No, just the visitor center. This one's original. Funny thing, though, Ms. Sadie was in here the other day and mentioned it felt cool. Are you catching a draft, Emma?" he asked.

"Yeah, I kind of am," I replied. "Funny, this time of year, isn't it?"

"It is. We might have a hole in one of the rafters. Some critter or other probably worked through the eaves, trying to find a place to build a nest. Drew Mabry does all the repair work for us. I'll have him send his boys out to take a look. Come on, let's head on to the next stop," he said as he stepped out through the door.

I went to follow him, and I could've sworn I heard a creak at the back of the room. I turned to look but didn't see anything. The cold chill ran up my spine again as I stepped out through the door and into the main courtyard.

We toured the stables, the armory, the mess building, which housed the Old Fort Café, and the grounds. Around the perimeter of the fort, Mr. Littman pointed out brass historical markers that described various battles, skirmishes, and guerrilla attacks by bands of Confederate militia throughout the fort's history. Each plaque was marked on the map he had given me, and he provided me with a packet that included the verbiage from each one.

"Now, here's another story for you, but nobody knows if this one is really true," he started as we walked back toward the visitor center. "Some of the townsfolk around here like to say it is, of course, what with so many of them having ancestors who fought, and died, right here in this fort alongside Stapleton and the others."

He paused, seemingly for dramatic effect, in the center of the courtyard.

"The story goes that Ulysses, U. S. Grant himself came right here to Hillbilly Hollow. The story says that he was here on his way to lay siege to Atlanta. While he was at the fort, a large group of rebel militia attacked. Grant and his men, along with Stapleton's forces, made short work of the rebels." He nodded, making a sweeping motion with his hand.

"I have to say, that story doesn't sound so unusual." I shrugged.

"No, that's not the unusual part. You see, Grant and Stapleton took part in the combat themselves. They fought right alongside their men. The story says that Grant ran the commander of the rebel forces clean through with his beloved saber. When the fighting was all said and done, though, the body of the rebel had been carried off, still impaled by Grant's sword. He was livid at the loss of his weapon, but as the hours dragged on, he had to get his troops moving. He left the saber behind, and as we all know, went on to lay siege to Atlanta."

"So, they never found the sword?" I asked.

"Well, that's the funny part. Supposedly, the troops found the man who had been impaled by Grant and retrieved the sword for him. They kept it here at the fort, expecting him to return, but he never did. The fate of Grant's saber is then simply lost to history. No one knows whatever became of it."

"Okay, they talk about history coming to life, but that is a pretty cool story," I replied.

He seemed pleased to have made the tour interesting for me.

Back at the visitor center, Mr. Littman showed me into his office, and we sat down. He pulled a couple of cans of pop from the mini fridge behind his desk and handed me one. "So, your first Old Fort Days will be coming up in about a week," he said, popping the top on the can and taking a gulp. "If you'll give Sadie your size, she'll get you your costume."

"I can give you my size," I replied, but he stopped me mid-sentence.

"Emma, I've been married for thirty-five years. I wouldn't have been if I didn't know better than to ask a lady what size dress she wears."

We both laughed.

"Now, you'll have your choice of jobs. We do have some ladies who take the role of a soldier," he paused, looking me up and down, "but with that long hair and a face as pretty as yours, you'd never pass for a boy." He shuffled through several pieces of paper. "Ah, here we go. We have several open slots for camp followers – those were the wives and other ladies who would stay at the encampment to do laundry, cook, and things like that."

I wrinkled my nose a bit, and he must've sensed that didn't sound particularly interesting.

"Important jobs, but nonetheless…here we go! How about a nurse? I have a slot open."

"Ooh, that sounds fun! I'll take it!" I smiled broadly and had a fleeting thought that Billy would probably try to correct me on what I should and shouldn't say or do in my role. "So do I have to do some training or something?"

"No, we'll go over everything with you Friday morning next week when you arrive. We get here early. Gates open at nine, and we're here by seven-thirty. Will you be able to make it?" he asked.

"Of course, no problem."

"Good. Oh, one other thing. On Monday night, we have the bi-weekly cleanup at four in the afternoon. All the society members come down, and we take bags through the whole site, make sure everything is clean and ready for guests at the weekend." He nodded to emphasize the last phrase.

"Got it! I'll be here!" I smiled and thanked Mr. Littman.

* * *

AFTER I LEFT, I texted Suzy to see if she wanted lunch. She asked me to pick up sandwiches at the sub shop inside Chapman's gas station, and I brought them to the store.

"So, how'd it go?" she asked in a sing-song voice as I entered.

"How'd what go?" I replied, mimicking her.

"You know! You and *Bil-ly*?" she asked, batting her eyelashes.

I rolled my eyes. "We're *friends,* Suzy, just like you and I are. Let. It. Go."

I sat on the stool behind the counter and handed her the sandwich I'd brought her.

"I just came from the old fort. Mr. Littman showed me around. Good to see him looking so well," I said.

"I suppose your grandma told you about Prudence?" she asked, taking a bite of her club sandwich.

"No, she didn't mention. Is she okay?" I replied, tucking into my turkey sub.

"Well, apparently, she was so distraught after the vigil, Margene had to give her a tranquilizer." She raised an eyebrow. "Word is, she kept saying 'I shouldn't have done it,' over and over. Now, what do you suppose *that* is all about?" she asked.

"Hm, that's pretty dramatic." I contemplated. "You don't think...I mean, she was in love with Preacher Jacob. Surely she wouldn't have hurt him, do you think?"

"No. I mean..." She stopped and thought for a moment. "I heard that she had finally come right out and told him she was in love with him just a few days before he died. It makes no sense. How do you kill someone you're in love with?"

"I dunno." I shrugged. "They say it's a thin line between love and hate, right? If he rejected her...what do you think?"

"Well, Billy did say he was strangled. And she's been playing the organ since she was about ten – strong hands, I'd imagine. Who knows? Maybe she snapped?" Suzy said.

We finished our lunch, and I went down to the historical society to give Sadie my size for the costume.

I could see Betty was in the back, fussing with something on the wall as I talked with Sadie. She finished getting my information, and I asked, "Can I pop back and let Mrs. Blackwood know how this morning went?"

I mustered up the cutest, most harmless expression I could.

"Um..." Sadie seemed to hesitate and then looked back to me. "You know what? Go on." She shrugged.

"Hi, Mrs. Blackwood," I said as I walked up to her. "Everything alright?"

"Blast!" she said as she set a large picture frame on the floor against the wall. "Hm? Oh, Emma! Yes, it's fine."

I looked at the frame she had set down and saw it was a

large photo of Preacher Jacob in his cavalry uniform with a small memorial plaque on the bottom of the frame. "Oh, is that a memorial? That's nice!" I said.

"It's too big! It's just ridiculous. I mean, where am I supposed to put this thing?" she said in an annoyed tone. My eyes grew big in surprise at her tone, and she must've caught the expression on my face. "I mean, there's just not a good place to put it," she backpedaled, "I mean to do it justice, of course." She narrowed her eyes and cast a glance in my direction.

"Of course," I agreed, not really sure how to react to her apparent callousness toward the man that everyone else in town loved. "I was just coming by to tell you about this morning…at the fort?"

"Oh, yes. Did Richard take good care of you?" she asked.

"Yes, he was great. He showed me around and told me all the stories about the fort. I was just stopping by to give Ms. Sadie my size for the costume," I said, smiling.

Sadie walked up. "Betty, I'm so sorry to interrupt," she said. "Drew Mabry's here to see you."

"Oh, yes, yes. Send him to my office," Betty replied. "Emma, I'll see you soon."

She walked off into her office, and Drew Mabry followed her.

I stopped back at the front counter to say goodbye to Sadie. "Boy, she seems like she's having a bad day, huh?" I said.

"She's been real worked up lately," Sadie said. "I mean before, you know, everything with Preacher Jacob, I thought she was getting a little nervous about the election."

"The election? Like for society president?" I asked.

"Oh, yes, there was talk that Preacher Jacob was going to be voted in, and Betty would be o-u-t!" She raised an eyebrow and gave a knowing nod.

"Really? So, she was pretty angry about that?" I asked.

"She was, but I don't know what her problem is now. She's just so cranky all the time," she said. "I mean, they argued about how to allocate funding for the fort, but with Preacher Jacob gone, now she can sway the other members to vote her way. Still, she just seems so, I don't know, on edge." Sadie crossed her arms and tapped her chin with her forefinger, then shrugged.

"*Hmpf.* Well, maybe she's just worried until they find the killer. I think it's got everyone a little nervous," I said. "Anyway, I'd better go. I'll see you later."

I wanted to get back to the house to see if there was anything Grandma and Grandpa needed help with, and to eat dinner with them.

I passed Billy's clinic on the way back to Suzy's, where I had parked. I thought about stopping by, but I wasn't sure I was quite ready to tell him about the stick-message from the morning, so I decided I'd talk to him later.

CHAPTER 15

I changed when I got back to the farm and helped Grandpa patch a couple of places on the fence around the pig pen.

Grandma made meatloaf for dinner, my favorite, and we all sat down and ate together. It reminded me of when I was a little girl. Grandpa had been right, she didn't seem to remember a thing about having been on the roof the night before, or even seem tired.

I helped her clean up from dinner, and decided I needed to do something fun to take my mind off of all the talk about Preacher Jacob, not to mention the stress of having seen him, or evidence of him, just about every day since I'd arrived.

"Whadya say, Snowball? Wanna go for a little walk?" I asked my sidekick.

She bleated in response, which I took as a yes.

I went up to the attic and rifled through my suitcase until I found the pocket flashlight I kept for emergencies.

Snowball and I took off to the right of the house, and around the back of the house Billy had grown up in next door. The path down to the pond was overgrown, so I was sure no one had been to the pond in a while. Snowball followed behind me, jumping over branches, and stopping on occasion to munch on a sprig of foliage here or there. It was a clear night, without any clouds, so the moon shone down enough for me to see where I was going once I got to the clearing.

Reconnect with a simpler time, Dr. Jenson's words echoed in my head as I approached the pond. Then I thought about what Billy had said, that I should get better, in time. It really did feel good to tell someone the whole story. I knew he wouldn't tell a soul. *All for one*, after all.

I could hear the croaking as I got to the edge of the water. I slid off my shoes and tucked my socks into them, leaving them at the edge of the path, and tiptoed over to the muddy water's edge. I heard croaking immediately to my left, so I turned on the little flashlight, and secured it between my teeth, then turned to spot a giant bullfrog in the tall grass at the edge of the mud.

I lunged, and missed, the fat frog leaping out of my grasp at the last minute.

"Sugar!" I exclaimed.

I heard another one nearby and turned to my right, just getting it by one foot.

Yeah! I giggled. *Maybe I've still got it!* I thought.

He was a good size, and if I was a frog-eating kind of girl, he would be big enough to take home.

"Off you go," I said quietly, letting him go.

I stepped around the edge of the pond and heard another. Turning, I had it spotted in the small circle of light emanating from my little flashlight. I moved slowly, and deliberately. Finally, I leaped forward, and as I did, I heard a loud *hoo*, which sounded like it was right behind my head. The frog hopped just beyond my grasp, and as it hit a log poking up out of the pond, a large owl swooped down and snatched it up.

I hit a slick rock as I stepped to the side away from the frog, and my foot slipped. I lost my footing and went straight down into the pond.

"Sugar!" I exclaimed, louder this time.

My entire front half was in the silty pond water, only my hair, the back of my shoulders, and my backside were spared. I carefully stood up and decided I had better wade in a bit and at least try to rinse off some of the mud.

I could be soaked, or I could be soaked and muddy – not much difference, I thought.

After I rinsed off, I walked back to where I had left my shoes. I picked the shoes up, and the sock was in one shoe, but not the other. I turned the flashlight on and looked around the area where my shoes had been. Still, no sock.

"What the heck?" I muttered as I continued to scan for my missing sock.

I heard a rustling sound, and as I looked around, I saw Snowball standing near me. Dangling from her mouth was my missing sock.

"Snowball! No!"

I leaned forward to take it away from her and grabbed the end. She dug her feet into the mud and set her jaw, holding on tight. After a moment, I gave up, and slipped my shoes on without the socks and headed back up to the house.

About halfway up the path, I veered off and took a shortcut I remembered that would take me to the field on our farm that overlooked the valley. When I got to the field clearing, I looked up, appreciating the stars in the night sky.

You don't see stars like this in New York, I thought.

I sat on the hillside with my feet outstretched, leaning back on my palms. Snowball plopped down beside me and rested her head on my leg. I scratched the top of her head, enjoying the peace and quiet.

A little while later, I got up and walked back to the house. I took my, by then, mostly-dry shoes off on the back porch, and quietly rinsed off in the laundry room. I went up to the attic and checked my phone before I lay down. I had one missed call and text, both from Billy.

BILLY: Just wanted 2 say hi. Glad we talked yesterday. Halee keeps looking 4 u by the firepit. I think u r stealing my dog. LOL Goodnight

ME: C u 2moro? Tell my new puppy friend goodnight.

BILLY: Goodnight Emma

As I LAY BACK, feeling a little more relaxed, a smile crept across my face. I was starting to feel like coming home to recuperate was the right decision.

* * *

I SPENT the day tending the garden with Grandma. She had a large patch of strawberries, which were my favorite thing from the garden, and birds kept picking off the fruit before they could ripen. She decided to build a sort of hutch around the patch with panels she could open from the top while she worked the patch, but that would be a deterrent for birds and deer.

I grabbed a few tools from the equipment shed and used a wheelbarrow to bring several stakes and some chicken wire. I used a small sledgehammer to drive each piece of stake into the ground, and we attached the chicken wire with a staple gun. We constructed frames from some slat board I found in the back of the barn to make the top, hinging it with wire at the back of each piece. It wasn't the prettiest bit of fencing on the farm, but it would definitely do the trick.

After the garden, we tended the pig sty and cleaned up the chicken coop. As we walked around the large habitat, I couldn't help but giggle as Grandma talked to the chickens and called them all by name. Where she got the idea to name them all after first ladies, I had no idea, but what really impressed me was how she could tell them all apart, even the ones with the same coloring.

"Okay, Emma, time to see to the goats," Grandma said after we had finished installing what I liked to refer to as the strawberry protection system.

She put the garden sheers in the pocket of her apron, and we loaded up the other supplies into the wheelbarrow, which I returned to the shed. Snowball, who had been watching the garden construction with interest, followed me to the shed, and over to the gated enclosure where Grandma had rounded up the rest of the goats. Snowball plopped down outside the fence before I opened the gates.

"Snowball too – grab her up, honey," Grandma said.

I picked up Snowball, carrying her like a baby, and she bleated her displeasure. Once inside the fence, I set her down and walked over to Grandma. There was a large oak barrel at the edge of the enclosure near the barn. She lifted one of the goats and set it up on top of the barrel, then grabbed the shears from her pocket.

"What…what are you doing?" I asked, terrified of the response.

"Gotta trim their hooves, dear. They walk on soft ground, and their hooves won't sharpen themselves. If we don't keep 'em trimmed, they could roll. Goats could go lame," she said.

"Oh, I see," I said, tentatively. I looked around for Snowball, who was crouched behind the other goats, hiding.

Grandma tucked an arm around the goat's backside and lifted its foot. With her free hand, she took the sheers and clipped off the excess hoof on one side and then the other. The goat didn't seem to be hurt by the process, but that didn't stop him from squirming. She repeated the process on the remaining three hooves, then patted the goat on the backside, and he leaped from the top of the barrel.

"Your turn, dear," she said turning to me and handing me the shears.

"Okay," I said.

I turned and picked up one of the smaller nanny goats and followed the process Grandma had. Overall, the little goat seemed no worse for wear, and I felt more confident. The next goat I worked on was less cooperative, and she kicked me hard in the ribs trying to get away. We did the rest of the flock, including Snowball, despite her attempts to hide.

I had texted Billy I'd stop by to see him and had to pick up my costume at the historical society, so I got cleaned up after chores and went to town. I stopped by the historical society, and by the time I made it to the clinic, Billy was locking up.

"Hey, Emma. I was startin' to think you wouldn't make it," he said walking out to reception to meet me.

"Sorry, I had a goat issue," I replied, rubbing my ribs.

"You want me to take a look?" he asked.

"Oh, no, no – I couldn't! I'm sure it's fine," I said, wincing a little. The thought of being examined by my friend made me a nervous wreck. "I've had broken ribs before, after all, and it didn't feel like this."

"The accident?" he asked.

I nodded my head.

"Well, different breaks can have different symptoms and feel different. Come on back, it'll only take a second," he said.

"It's low, so you don't even get to wear the fancy paper gown." He winked.

"Well, it does kinda hurt," I replied.

He waved me back into one of the exam rooms, and I hopped up on the little table.

Billy washed his hands, and I carefully lifted my shirt on the side just enough to expose the bottom rib, holding the fabric close around me to avoid any embarrassing wardrobe malfunctions. He looked at the bruise then, using two fingers, pressed gingerly on the bruise and the area around it.

"Tell me where it's tender," he said. He pressed in concentric circles, ending in the center of the bruise.

"Yowch!" I exclaimed.

He pressed a bit harder and rubbed his fingers along the rib.

"There's no sign of a break," he said, washing his hands again. "When you have a contusion over the bone, it's going to be more sensitive. You should be fine in a few days."

He took a prescription pad out of the drawer and jotted something on it.

"Here you go," he said, handing me a prescription slip.

I looked at the paper.

"Billy, this says cheeseburger and french fries," I said.

"Yep, and a milkshake, if you promise to follow doctor's orders and be careful with that side for a couple of days." He winked. "I thought we might pick up dinner and have it outside at my place. It's a nice night, and Halee would love to see you." He gave me that charming smile he always flashed when he was trying to get his way.

"You know what? That actually sounds pretty good," I replied. "Tell you what – go take care of the pup, and I'll grab the burgers and be at your place in a few. You won't have to bring me back to my truck."

He agreed, and I went over to the diner to pick up burgers, fries, and shakes.

When I got to Billy's, he had changed out of his khakis and button-down into jeans and a t-shirt.

"Come on in, Emma," he said when he answered the door.

We went to the backyard, and rather than sitting around the fire pit, we sat at the patio table and chairs up on the deck. I had barely put my purse down when Halee came and put her paws up on my leg for me to pick her up. I kneeled down to pat her on the head, telling her I'd pick her up after we ate dinner.

"Anything interesting happen at the clinic today?" I asked as we tucked into our burgers.

"Not anything you'd want me to talk about over dinner," he grinned. "Small town medicine is mundane and often, pretty gross."

"Thanks for not sharing, I think!" I giggled. "Speaking of small-town medicine…I know you can't tell me about somebody else's medical situation, but…well, I'm a little worried about my Grandma," I said.

"What's wrong? Do we need to get her in to see me?" he asked.

"Well, that's just it. I don't know – she might've been in to see you already." I scanned his face for any sign of affirmation.

"Well, you're right, I can't talk details, but if you're worried about her, maybe is there something I should be on the lookout for?" he asked, an expression of earnest concern on his face.

"It's just…the other night…well, Grandpa said it was nothing." I shrugged.

"Emma." He gave me that official doctor expression of his. It was very dad-like and off-putting. "What's goin' on?"

"The other night, something woke me up. I went outside

and found Grandpa retrieving Grandma from the roof. She was up there…well, singing." I looked at him sheepishly.

"Singing?" He chuckled. "Maybe she was looking for better acoustics?"

"Come on, this is serious! She's seventy – she could've gotten hurt." I shook my head at him.

"I'm sorry," he said, flipping back into medical mode. "You're right of course. Was she confused, or did she seem in distress?"

"Not really. Grandpa says this sometimes happens for about four nights, then she's right back to normal."

"You know, Emma, people cope with stress in lots of ways. This may not have started until the past few years, but this could be her body's strange way of helping her cope. She did lose your dad, after all. I mean, they were your parents, I don't mean to diminish that," he said almost apologetically. "But at the same time, that was her son. People don't expect to bury a child. She's been a strong woman our whole lives. Maybe this is just her outlet. People find amazing ways to cope with stress and trauma," he said.

Yeah, like seeing imaginary messages composed of twigs, I thought.

I changed the subject. "Hey, did I tell you I went bull frogging the other night?"

"Really?" he asked, raising an eyebrow. "And, how did you do?"

"I'm not fast," I replied. "I might have ended up wearing some mud, and not in the glamorous spa experience kind of way."

We both laughed.

We chatted over dinner about this and that and moved over to the lounge chairs around the fire pit after we ate. As soon as I reclined back in the chair, Halee hopped up beside me and snuggled into my lap. I scratched behind her ears, and she wriggled her backside, wagging her little tail.

"See? You're stealing my dog. Some friend you are, you furry little traitor!" He glared at Halee and chuckled.

"Well, Snowball's going to be mad when she smells you on me," I said to the pup.

"You got a dog?" Billy asked.

"Not exactly," I replied. "She's a goat." I giggled.

I had to think whether I should tell Billy about the letters I saw on the ground. He was my oldest friend, after all. He had been great when I told him about the visions, and I had no reason not to believe he would help me work through this as well. I must've been deeper in thought than I realized.

"Well, I see that my prescription for a milkshake didn't help. Are your ribs still hurting?" Billy asked, looking a little concerned.

"Huh? Oh! No, I'm okay. I was just thinking," I replied.

"Thinking about…?" He gave me a quizzical look.

I sighed and wriggled to take my phone out of my back pocket without disturbing Halee. "Thinking about whether I should show you this." I clicked open the photo I had snapped and handed him my phone.

"Is this some sort of outsider art therapy or something?" he asked.

"Not quite. I found that in the grass near the outhouse. Just like you see it – I didn't touch a thing."

I could tell he was trying to process what I'd just said.

"I mean, it's letters, right? U-S? I'm not crazy, am I?"

"You've always been a little crazy, Emma," he said, "but not because of this. It definitely says U-S. Or *us* maybe. What do you think it means?"

"I'm not sure, but I think it's a clue to whatever these ghosts or visions or whatever they are might be trying to tell me."

CHAPTER 16

$\mathcal{I}$t was Saturday morning – the day of Preacher Jacob's funeral. Fortunately, among the things I had packed in my suitcase was a black dress. If there was anything that my time in New York had taught me, it was that one should always have a little black dress, attractive, yet conservative, to be prepared for any occasion. I hated that this was the occasion for which I needed it, but at the same time, I was glad I could dress appropriately for the funeral.

I went downstairs and had breakfast with Grandma and Grandpa.

"Mornin', Emma, dear," Grandma said. "How's your side?"

"Not too bad, thanks. I had Billy take a look yesterday afternoon. It's just a bruise," I replied, kissing Grandpa on the cheek as I sat down.

"What's the matter?" Grandpa asked. He was less gruff than he usually was, which I put down to his preparing himself to make conversation with everyone at the funeral.

"Trimmin' hooves," Grandma replied before I could. "Samson got her in the ribs," she said.

Grandpa looked me up and down. "Well, I bet you know

how to hold 'em next time, dontcha?" He held up his paper, but I could see the grin behind it.

"Pain's a powerful teacher, Grandpa," I replied, grinning back.

* * *

MY MUSCLES HAD BEEN SORE for the previous few days from all the chores I had been helping with all week. The team cycling fitness classes I had been taking in my flatiron neighborhood had not prepared me for the level of bending, stretching and lifting I had done this week. I took a nice, hot bath before I got ready to go to the funeral. The water smarted when it hit my ribs, but after a moment, the heat felt good on my tired arms, legs, and back.

I added some makeup, including waterproof mascara in case I cried, which I suspected I might. Even if I didn't know the person well, I always felt so bad for the family who were left behind, missing their loved one. I thought of my parents, and kissed the pads of my index and middle fingers, and flipped them toward the sky.

I straightened my hair and put on the black dress with a pair of black pumps. When I got downstairs, Grandpa had on his charcoal gray suit, and Grandma was wearing a black dress with a thin, three-quarter-sleeved jacket over the top, and her pearls. It suddenly occurred to me that they had these clothes at the ready. At their age, I shouldn't have been surprised. I wondered how many friends, classmates, and acquaintances they had buried over the past decade. I was suddenly incredibly grateful I had come home, even if the reasons were selfish. I kissed Grandma on the cheek, careful not to ruin her makeup.

"You look beautiful," I said. I winked at Grandpa. "And you clean up nicely too."

We took the car into town, and when we arrived, the church parking lot was already full. Grandpa dropped off Grandma and me and went to park down by the diner.

As soon as we got out of the car, Grandma was besieged by ladies of a similar age, all of whom had been in the town their whole lives. Jackie Colton, Suzy's Mom, found her and they made their way to look for Margene Huffler, who was undoubtedly trying to keep Prudence from falling to pieces.

I saw Suzy and Brian coming down the sidewalk and paused to wait for them. When Suzy got close, I looped my elbow through hers.

"How you holding up?" I asked, seeing that she was emotional.

"I'm okay. I mean, we weren't super close – we didn't all socialize or anything, but I still can't believe it," she said.

"Me too. I told you guys, I had just seen him," Brian added. "It seems like just yesterday my Grandpa retired and Preacher Jacob took over. He was such a good man – Grandpa was completely confident handing the reins over to him."

We all walked into the church, and I saw all the little factions of townspeople form as everyone greeted each other before the service. Grandma's quilting circle were all gathered around a completely bereft Prudence Huffler. Mayor Teller, Jim Stinnett from the First National Bank, and Sam Puckett, the town attorney everyone simply called Puck, were huddled up in a corner, undoubtedly talking business.

The actual mayor – the current one – Mayor Bigsby, was near the church doors, and Tucker was right next to him in his dress uniform. He was greeting everyone as they came in. Betty Blackwood sat in the front pew on one side of the church, surrounded by Mr. Littman, Sadie Cooper, Vernon Dykstra, and a few other people I recognized as board members for the historical society. It dawned on me that, with no family, Preacher Jacob would be attended by his church family and the members of the historical society in which he had spent most of his time.

On the opposite front bench sat Prudence Huffler. She seemed in a daze, and I wondered if Billy had prescribed something to calm her. Just as I was thinking how composed she was, she stood, zombie-like, and took a few steps forward. Margene, Grandma, and the others had busied themselves talking to the last quilting circle members to arrive and didn't notice her. I patted Suzy's arm and pointed to the front, careful not to draw attention. I felt a hand on my shoulder and turned to see Billy.

"Uh-oh," he said before he could sit down. He quickly began walking toward the front of the church.

Prudence ascended the two steps up to the stage where the lectern usually stood. On this day, the lectern was instead on the floor level, and on the stage was Preacher Jacob, his large casket flanked by huge wreaths and large sprays of flowers. By the time Prudence got to the casket itself, Billy was as far as the front pew. He hastened his pace but was not fast enough to stop the scene that started to unfold.

"Why? Whyyy?" Prudence wailed, reaching into the casket, grabbing Preacher Jacob's lapels. "I shouldn't have done it! I shouldn't have! Why?" She moaned and sobbed, her lanky frame bent over into the casket in a futile embrace of the dead man.

Grandma, Margene, and the others turned, gasping. Grandma literally clutched her pearls at the sight.

Billy, though, was already upon Prudence when the assembled mourners began to react to her outcry. I couldn't hear what he was saying from where we sat, but he had grasped her by the shoulders and stood her upright. He was whispering into her ear as he walked her off of the stage and back to her seat in the first pew. He kneeled in front of her, one hand on her knee as if he meant to pin her to the seat. I saw him take something from his jacket pocket, and motion to Margene, who disappeared, returning a moment later with a bottle of water. He handed to Prudence what must've been a pill of some kind, followed by the bottle of water.

Standing, he grasped her shoulder, patting it firmly, and said something to Margene before he walked back to his seat beside me.

As he sat beside me in the pew, I looked up at him, eyebrow raised.

"Well, that was impressive," I said.

He unbuttoned his jacket and sat back in the seat, putting an arm around me. I gazed at his hand, which was flopped around my shoulder, then looked up at him inquiringly.

He leaned to me and whispered, "Sherrie just walked in. Give a guy a break will ya?" He sat upright then continued. "I just told Prudence that she had to pull herself together. What can I say? People listen to doctors." He shrugged.

"Some people do, I guess," I replied with a smug grin.

Suzy had been engrossed in conversation with Brian and turned to look at me, and immediately saw Billy's hand on my shoulder. She gave me a self-satisfied look and grinned. I tried to be inconspicuous as I crooked my thumb toward Sherrie Selby, who had just sat down across from us.

"Mm-hmm, sure," Suzy whispered.

We may have all been out of college and thirty-some-thing, but sitting across the pew casting looks at each other and whispering, I felt like we were right back in high school at one of those interminable assemblies.

The music began, and the service started. Danny Baxter did the preaching, and Mr. Littman did the main eulogy, then several of the town elders also got up and spoke. Prudence didn't make a scene again but sobbed quietly throughout the service. As I looked around the chapel, I saw Betty Blackwood sitting upright, stiff as a board, looking not so much sad as stoic. Mayor Teller, who Preacher Jacob had been in some sort of heated exchange with just before his death, sat, leaning his back against the pew, arms folded across his ample belly. Prudence was a shell of a woman, held by her mother and my Grandma who had her propped up on either side.

Those three, I thought, *those are the only ones who had any motive to hurt him.*

I hated to admit it, but I tuned out the rest of the service. My mind kept going back to the things I had seen. Preacher Jacob pointing toward the fort, almost beckoning me to follow him. The sticks that spelled out U-S. Preacher Jacob's ghost again pointing toward the old fort, leaning forward, then collapsing.

As I thought about that motion – leaning forward and collapsing to the floor, a chill ran up my spine. I had a revelation, and I suddenly knew how to find out just who had killed him.

CHAPTER 17

*a*fter the service, Preacher Jacob was laid to rest in the church graveyard. Only his closest friends, and the town elders attended the graveside. The rest of the congregation and townspeople who didn't regularly attend church milled around in the fellowship hall. The ladies' charitable society had put on quite a spread with everything from casseroles to fried chicken.

Suzy, Brian, and Billy got plates and sat at one of the large, round tables. I grabbed a pop but thought I had better make the rounds instead of sitting with my friends.

"Be right back," I told them when I spied Tucker come in from outside. I made a beeline for him.

"Hi, Tucker," I said as I strode up to him.

"Emma," he said, touching the brim of his hat.

"The service was really beautiful," I said, leaning in closer.

I could see several of the single women in town keeping a close eye on me as we spoke. Tucker was certainly handsome, especially in his dress uniform, but my interest in him was purely theatrical.

"It was. Such a shame to put a good man in the ground

well before his time." He shook his head and crossed his arms.

"You know," I put my fingertips on his forearm and leaned in closer still, "I was thinking how hard all of this must be on you and your men."

"Well, it's been a rough few days, I reckon," he looked down, then back up at me. "But protecting and serving is what we do. Gotta make sure these folks are safe what with a killer runnin' around." He nodded as if to himself.

"Well, I, for one, sleep a lot better at night knowing you and your men are on the case," I said.

His humble smirk relaxed into a full smile, beaming down on me with warmth and pride.

I smiled back and broached my next question. "So, Tucker." I brought my voice down to a whisper so he'd have to lean in to hear me. "Do you think it was someone here today? I always hear that criminals like to return to the scene of the crime, and, well, a funeral is pretty close to doing that."

He looked a little bewildered for a moment as if he hadn't thought of the possibility that the killer could be in the same room with us at that very moment. Then, he regained his composure and leaned in, almost whispering in my ear, "Don't you worry, Emma. There's a few people I got my eye on. My boys are on the lookout for anything strange." He winked at me and gave me a quick pat on the back. "We've got it covered."

"Oh, that does make me feel better. Thanks, Tucker." I touched his arm again and walked off. I caught Billy and Suzy both giving me a glare, but I didn't have time for damage control. Someone else had been watching my interaction with Tucker, and that's who I needed to speak to next.

I walked over to the biggest gossip in town – the one woman who wouldn't hurt a soul, but who traded in gossip like the Native Americans who first settled this land had traded fur pelts.

"Hi, Grandma," I said, sitting down next to her.

"Hello, Emma. I saw you talking to Tucker. Everything alright?" she asked sweetly.

"Oh, yes. I was just asking him…" I looked around, feigning the need for privacy for what I was about to say next, and leaned in. "…about the case. You know, if they were any closer to catching Preacher Jacob's killer?"

"Oh! Is that right? And…what did he say?" she asked.

"Oh, you won't believe it!" I leaned closer still. "He said that they had a new piece of evidence. Apparently, the murderer left a clue at the scene of the crime. He said that he wanted to make sure everything was orderly while folks paid their respects today, but tomorrow, they're going back to the scene with a forensic team to recover the evidence!" I leaned back a little and nodded my head knowingly.

"You don't say! My goodness!" she replied. "Did he say what it was?"

"No, he said that's all confidential police business, but whatever it is, he said it positively identifies the killer." I nodded as she put her hand up to her mouth in surprise.

"Well, how do you like that? A killer right here in Hillbilly Hollow! I never – I mean I really never!" She shook her head.

"But Grandma, you mustn't tell anyone I told you. I don't want to get in trouble for interfering with a police investigation, you understand." I smiled. "Anyway, I'm going to go sit with Suzy, Brian, and Billy for a bit. I'll get one of them to bring me home. Talk to you later."

I went back to the table where my friends had finished with their lunch. "What was all that about?" Billy started as soon as I sat down.

"Oh, nothing," I replied.

"Nothing? I gotta say, you and Tucker looked pretty chummy, Emma," Suzy added.

"Are you kidding? As if! No – I was just talking to him about Preacher Jacob," I replied.

"Emma, you really should be careful. If one of these folks is really, you know, responsible…just think what they'd do to you if they catch you poking your nose in where it doesn't belong. If something happened to you…" Billy trailed off.

"Nothing's going to happen to me." I shrugged. "I just wanted to find out if they had any real leads."

He looked at me with that stern, doctor's expression, and I suspected he knew why I wanted to know so badly how the investigation was going.

As I sat at the table, I watched as my plan took root. During the service, I'd had the idea to spread the word that the killer had left something behind. Who better to tell than my grandma? I loved her dearly, and she wouldn't hurt a fly, but that woman loved a good story! I saw her go from table to table, stopping to talk with Sadie, who immediately told Betty. Betty looked concerned. She might have just been upset at the idea of further investigations at the fort. Or, she could've been the killer. After all, Billy said he was strangled from behind, and I saw Preacher Jacob's ghost pantomime being bent over, surprised, and succumbing to the strangulation. Betty Blackwood wasn't a big woman, but the element of surprise and the leverage of standing over a man who was bent down might have given her the advantage.

I saw Grandma talking to Margene and Prudence. Prudence seemed to have a hard time registering what Grandma was saying, but Margene was visibly shocked. She leaned over and whispered into Prudence's ear, and a fresh round of tears started to flow from Prudence's eyes as she sobbed into her handkerchief. She might have killed him in a fit of jealous rage when Preacher Jacob rejected her. Realizing her crime, she could be overcome with remorse. She did keep saying, "I shouldn't have done it." I wondered if she meant the confession of her love for Preacher Jacob, or the murder.

Grandma walked around and talked to a few other people, but what I saw next was surprising. Brian had told Tucker that he saw Preacher Jacob and Mayor Teller get into a verbal altercation at Teller's antique shop just a few days before the murder. Still, Tucker didn't seem the slightest bit suspicious of our former mayor. I never saw Grandma speak to him. Sadie Cooper, however, got up a few minutes after talking to Grandma and made her way to the hallway between the kitchen and rectory. As she walked by Mayor Teller, I saw her just barely graze his arm, and a moment later, he followed her. I could just see them out of the corner of my eye without being too obvious, but they talked for several minutes, and it looked like he had taken her hand in his. Someone obstructed my view, and a moment later, Sadie was coming out of the hallway without Mayor Teller anywhere in sight.

I could've been wrong, but I was sure one of these three people was responsible, one way or another, for Preacher Jacob's death. The old fort was closed for the funeral, and I intended to get there just about nightfall to see if the murderer had taken the bait and returned to the scene of the crime.

CHAPTER 18

*W*e spent the rest of the afternoon at Suzy's house. Suzy and I talked about her wedding plans, and Brian and Billy watched baseball. As the late afternoon wore on, I knew I had to get back to the farm. Billy offered to drop me off, and we headed out to the edge of town.

"Emma, I'm serious," Billy said when he dropped me off. "Just promise me you'll be careful. Don't do anything risky or stupid, okay?"

"Billy, seriously – I can take care of myself," I said, then put on my thickest fake New York accent. "I'm practically a New Yorkah! Fuggedaboudit!" We both laughed.

"That was genuinely the worst New York accent I ever heard." He gave me a quick hug. "G'night, Emma," he said, then turned back. "Text me tomorrow, okay?"

I went to the front door and acted as if I were unlocking it until he got down the driveway. I had wanted to change, but it was starting to get dark, and I had to get to the fort before night fell. I threw my house keys back in my bag and dug out the key to the farm truck. I waited two more minutes until I was sure Billy would be past the turnoff for the fort and started down the highway toward town.

When I got to the old fort, the wooden CLOSED sign was up, but there was nothing blocking the entrance. I drove in quietly and turned off my headlights. I pulled the truck around the end of the armory building, out of sight. Grabbing my phone, I stepped out of the truck and carefully pushed the door shut until it just clicked.

I walked around the back of the armory building until I got to the barracks. There was no sign of anyone, so, cautiously, I crept inside. I got a cold chill as soon as I stepped into the building, just as I had before when Mr. Littman had shown me around.

I thought I heard a noise at the back of the barracks near a gun rack, and walked back, staying quiet, just in case. I didn't see anything. I walked over to the cannonball on the stand in the corner and looked back to the dent in the floor. A few seconds could have made all the difference. If Commander Stapleton had slept just a few minutes longer, or that shot had misfired just a few minutes sooner, he would've been a goner. The sign on the display stand read, "Stapleton's Cannonball," but I thought that was wrong. It hadn't been Stapleton's. If it had struck him, the fort might have fallen to rebel advances. Who knew? So many skirmishes and battles could have come out differently. But it didn't do him in – it missed him.

My hand instinctively went to the spot on my head where my skull had connected with the hood of the taxi.

If I had walked a minute slower, I thought, *that taxi might have been going fast enough to do some real damage. A minute faster and I could've been through the crosswalk without incident.*

Then I thought about Preacher Jacob. What had he been doing here so late that night? What had he been bending down for? If he had come earlier or later, he might not have run into his killer.

Again, I heard the sound, almost like creaking floorboards. I started to investigate once more, but heard something outside. After a moment, I realized it was the sound of tires on gravel. There were some mattresses stood up along the right side wall, so I hid behind them. As the headlights shone through the window, they illuminated the gun rack. At the very bottom, on the facing, I saw a small carving. It was two letters. U-S.

I heard a door slam. *A car,* I thought, *not a truck.*

In another moment, whoever it was had entered the building.

I held my breath as a narrow beam of light pierced the darkness of the room, sweeping back and forth. I heard the sound of footfalls growing closer. They passed by me, and I breathed a silent sigh of relief.

I couldn't see the figure in the dark but heard the clanging of metal as they pulled swords from the weapons rack, one by one. They seemed to hold each one for a few minutes before replacing it hastily as if aggravated.

What could they be looking for? I wondered.

I tried to peer further around the corner of the mattress without shifting it and giving away my location. It was no use – I couldn't see who it was.

Again, I heard the creaking of floorboards near the weapons rack as I had heard before, and felt a chill.

"Who's there?" I heard a man say. "I said, *who's there!*" He said it again, angrier, this time.

I made myself as small as I could. Luckily, he didn't see me.

"Old fool," he said to himself. "Getting jumpy!" I heard the electronic *swish* of a phone being activated then the sound of dialing.

"I thought you said it was here!" he said angrily. "Yes, I have looked. Yes, *at all of them!*" He muttered something under his breath that sounded vaguely like an expletive. "You said...*YOU said it would be here!*" He paced back and forth for another minute or two, listening to the person on the other end of the line. "Okay. Okay, I'll keep looking. I've gotta go."

With a *click*, I knew he was finished with his call. He seemed beyond frustrated that he couldn't find whatever he was searching for, and walked over to the weapons rack, leaning his hands on the railing.

Wait, is that...is that a pinky ring? I asked myself as I looked at the thick fingers grasping the railing of the weapons rack. *Is that...*

My train of thought was interrupted as the figure kicked the base of the wooden rack. As he did, the front facing fell down.

He gave an angry yell. Then he bent down with a heaving breath, to try to put the piece of wood back. After all, murderers who creep around in barracks in the middle of the night looking for evidence they've left behind certainly don't want to be given away by having damaged the scene of the crime.

He was turned away, and I still couldn't see his face, but I could tell he was a larger man, and he moved as if he were older. As he got down on all fours to assess the damage, I got an unfortunate view of his backside, along with the soles of what looked to be quite expensive cowboy boots.

"Well, well, well...what have we here?" he said, a note of glee in his voice as his hand disappeared under the weapons rack. I heard the scraping of metal against wood as he pulled the item out.

With a great deal of effort, he stood up, moving closer to the window on the other side of the barracks. Light glinted off the item as, presumably, he moved it back and forth in the glow from the headlights. I heard his phone click again.

"You won't believe it," he said into the phone. "I did. It's… it's so much more beautiful than I could've even imagined!" He continued, "Oh yes, six figures at least…They are – his initials are right here on the hilt. U-S-G."

USG? I wasn't sure what it meant, but I was certain it had to do with the letters near the outhouse.

It sounded as though my suspect was beginning to taper off his phone conversation. I might have a few minutes while he made repairs to the board he had kicked loose, but he would be gone soon, and I still wasn't sure who it was. As he hung up the phone, I decided to text Billy to get Tucker down here to arrest him. First, though, I decided I had better try to snap a photo in case he left before they arrived.

Cautiously, I slid my phone open, making sure it was on silent mode and set to airplane mode to be sure I didn't get a call that would give me away. I slid the edge of the phone, camera side out, just about half an inch from the edge of the mattress. I tried to zoom in on the little screen to see if I could tell, for certain, who it was, but it was just too dark. My heart pounded, and my breath was ragged. Each time I inhaled, the goat-shaped bruise on my side hurt more. I finally summoned up all of my courage and hit the button to snap a picture.

As my phone came to life, the color drained from my face.

"What? Who's there?" The man's voice boomed in the empty building as the pinpoint of light from my phone's flash illuminated his face, giving away my location.

The shutter clicked just as he turned around, and there, on my phone, was a clear photo of Mayor Teller, holding an antique saber.

He took a lumbering step toward me, and I slid out the other side of the mattresses, putting one of the bunks between us for protection. He stood at the opposite end of the bunk, but I was too far for him to reach. I stepped around the other end, and he struggled to get closer.

"Emma, I don't know what you think is going on here, but it's nothing. Nothing, do you hear me? Let's talk about this. We can work this all out." His teeth were showing, but it was less of a smile and more of a growl.

"I know it was you!" I snapped. "I know you killed Preacher Jacob!"

"What are you talking about? Why, I was just here checking on the place. With a murderer running around, folks can't be too careful. Just because I'm no longer the mayor, doesn't mean I don't feel a deep responsibility to the people of this town!"

"Are you kidding me? I'm the one who started the rumor that the killer left something behind. I was waiting to see who would show up, and here you are!"

I jumped back, stepping behind another set of bunks. It was hard to keep my footing on the uneven hardwood floors, especially in heels, but if he got his hands on me, there was no telling what he might do. I fumbled with my phone, trying to call 911 or text someone, but it wouldn't work.

"I don't know what rumor you're talkin' about, Ms. Hooper. Now, one rumor I did hear, and I heard it from your own grandma. I heard you hit your head back in the city and came home to recuperate. Maybe you aren't thinkin' too clear." He shook his head menacingly.

"Oh yeah?" I said, taking another step backward. "Well that hardly matters because I have a picture of you stealing that old sword!"

Sugar! Why did I tell him that? He's never going to let me out of here now!

But I couldn't stop myself from asking, "Is that thing what you killed Preacher Jacob over? Some rusty old relic?"

My comment ignited something. In the light pooling in from his car, I could see his pale gray brows furrowed into a deep V, and his complexion turned crimson. I had made him very angry.

"You have no *idea* what this is!" he exclaimed. "This is not some *rusty old relic*, as you say. This sword belonged to none other than Ulysses S. Grant himself! He lost it in a skirmish at this very site! By the time Stapleton's men found it, he was down around Savannah, burning the path that would clear the way to this country's reunification!" He thrust the sword into the air for emphasis.

I continued trying to get my phone to work, and again, he lunged toward me. This time, I backed up farther, beyond the last bunk. When he lunged again, I jumped back with my legs wide, trying to gain some stability. The thrust of the sword went right between my knees, slicing through my dress like butter. The proximity was terrifying.

As I leaped backward, all I could think of was to stall for time. "Why did Preacher Jacob have to die?" I demanded.

That slowed him down for a moment. He hefted the sword, as if considering whether to give me an answer. He must've decided the truth couldn't do him any harm, since I was about to be dead.

He said, "That fool didn't understand what he'd found! He came down to the antique shop and described the sword to me, but then he wouldn't sell it. He wanted it to stay at the fort. Wouldn't even tell me where it was! I arranged to meet him here that night to examine the sword for authenticity, but things went wrong. It was only after I killed him that I realized he still hadn't told me exactly where the sword was, only that it was somewhere in the fort. I couldn't look for it right then. I panicked and cleared out." He tilted his head to one side, as he remembered the events of that night.

Then he continued, "But once I heard I'd left a clue to my

identity behind, it seemed like a good time to beat the police here. Find whatever the evidence was and look for the sword again at the same time. It was Sadie who got the idea the sword would be in plain sight in the weapons rack."

The explanation had made him pause for a moment, but now he was advancing once more.

I stepped back again, and my high heel hit the dent in the floor, causing me to tumble backward. My phone flew out of my hand, just out of reach as I tried to use my palms to crawl away in a crab walk.

Teller reached me, standing over me with the sword in his hand.

"Help! Help!" I screamed at the top of my lungs, desperate for anyone to hear my pleas.

"Sorry, darlin,' but that won't help you. A city ordinance has kept anyone from building within a thousand yards of the fort. An ordinance that *I* passed through as mayor. All the good I did for this city over the years, but these people don't appreciate anything! They run me out of town for making a few deals that are in my favor. How's that for gratitude!" He shook his head at the past injury of having to step down from office.

"No matter, though," he said, a smile creeping across his face. "This sword, the very one that my own three-times great granddaddy pulled out of the gut of a rebel traitor, is worth a small fortune. I'm going to sell it and head off to South America, where my type of skills are appreciated!"

"So that's what this was all about? Money?" I asked, trying again to buy time until I could figure out what to do.

"Of course it was about money, you stupid girl! Why does anyone do what they do? Two reasons: love or money. Sometimes both. Well, I'm gonna have both, but first, I have to take care of an unexpected problem." He raised the sword over his head.

"Please, please, please," I muttered as I shut my eyes tight. "Somebody – anybody! Help me!"

I could've sworn I heard the creak of floorboards behind me as a cold shiver ran across my skin.

Out of nowhere, the pedestal in the corner, the one upon which Stapleton's cannonball was perched, tipped forward. The cannonball went flying, landing squarely in the middle of Teller's shoulders.

He let out a pained *oomph* as he fell. The sword flew out of his hand, sliding across the floor, out of his grasp. I quickly stood and grabbed it in one hand, my cell phone in the other.

Teller lay on the ground, writhing in pain, barely conscious. I tried my phone again, finally remembering it had been in airplane mode. I dialed 911 and told the dispatcher where I was. Next, I texted Billy.

ME: Old fort – bring your doc kit – i'm ok

BILLY: ?! B right there

I stood over Teller with the sword in my hand, though I wasn't sure what I planned to do with it if he suddenly recovered. A few minutes later, the sheriff's department cars came roaring into the fort parking lot, sending gravel flying. Billy was right behind them in his truck.

After the police burst in, everything happened quickly.

Tucker took the sword from me, and he and one of the deputies I didn't know pulled me aside to take my statement. I explained how I had spread the rumor about the piece of evidence, then waited to see who would show up.

"That was a very foolish thing to do, Emma," Tucker said. "It was very dangerous, and I won't have vigilantes out here runnin' around, ya understand?" He was scolding me as if I were a child. Apparently, he had forgotten that we were only three years apart. He told the deputy to go shut off Teller's car and have it impounded as evidence. After he walked off, Tucker leaned in close. "But...even though that was foolish, it *did* help us find the killer. So, thanks, I guess." He winked and touched the front of his hat as he tipped his head to me slightly before walking away to check on the rest of the deputies' activities.

I sat on one of the cots as Billy finished examining Teller. After he was through, the deputies handcuffed Teller and put him in the car. Billy immediately came to where I was sitting. He squatted down in front of me.

"Are you alright? Did you get hurt? Anything I need to check?"

I shook my head no. "I fell on my backside, but that's about it. I'm fine, Billy, really."

"You do realize how mad I am at you right now, don't you?" he asked.

"Probably?" I shrugged playfully, but he was still frustrated.

"What if you had gotten yourself hurt? Or worse? Can you imagine me having to roll up on a crime scene with you as the victim? I'd...I'd..." He stopped and took my hands, pulling me to my feet, and hugged me tightly. "There's no such thing as two musketeers, ya know. It'd be impossible. We need to keep you around for a while." He stepped back and looked me up and down. "By the way, I didn't notice that vent in your skirt before. It's kind of ridiculous."

I looked down at the slash in the fabric and rolled my eyes. "What are you, a fashion critic now?" We both laughed.

Tucker gave me the okay to leave, and I headed back to the farm and went to bed.

CHAPTER 19

*T*he following morning, I told Grandma and Grandpa what had happened. They were shocked at the events of the night before but proud of me for trying to do the right thing. I also decided to tell them the truth – the whole truth – about my accident and the after effects of my brain injury.

"So, you see," I said as we spoke, "the doctor in New York thought it was just some sort of electrical impulses, misfiring in the brain. He said if I took it easy, went someplace where I could rest and recuperate, I'd get better."

"Well, Emma, now I don't know about all that. Seein' ghosts and such," Grandpa said in a serious tone.

"You mean – you mean you don't believe me?" I asked, incredulously. I had just poured out my heart, told them my whole story. I couldn't believe that he would doubt my sincerity.

"Oh, no. I believe you see the ghosts and whatnot. I'm just not sure some rest will make a difference. My cousin John, he got kicked in the head by a mule on his farm. Probably about your age, come to think," he said. "Anyway, he said the same as you. After a few days he started seein', well, spirits, he called 'em. Not all the time, but a lot of the time."

"What?" I asked, unable to believe what I was hearing. "Someone in our family got kicked in the head, and started seeing ghosts, and I'm just now hearing about this?"

"Your great-grandpa too, dear," Grandma said, retrieving a book from the cabinet under the television. She pulled out a photo of Grandpa with his sister, brother, and parents when they were young. "Yes, yes. Old Hooper was trying to put some water in his radiator on the side of the road, so he said. Anyway, got burned with the steam. He jumped back, tripped, and fell right on a rock the size of his head. After that, he seemed like he was talkin' to himself sometimes. Your great-grandmother Esther said he talked about seein' all sorts of specters and apparitions from time to time after that."

"Wow. Well, if I'd known about all that, I might've told you sooner," I said.

"No matter," Grandpa said. "I'm glad you told us anyway." He smiled, then winced suddenly.

"Grandpa, are you okay?" I asked, worriedly.

"He's fine!" Grandma said dismissively, returning the photo album to its proper place. "He pulled his shoulder picking up a bale of hay like he knows he ought not to do." She gave him a glare. "I think he was tryin' to impress someone," she said, looking at me.

"Grandpa! I wish I had known! You know I would've helped," I replied.

"Well, we Hoopers are a stubborn lot. None of us likes to admit when we need help, seems like." He smiled at me, and I blushed, realizing what he meant.

I hugged and kissed them both before I went down to town to talk with Suzy. She had help in the shop, so we spent the afternoon at her place catching up. After I finished regaling her with tales of my daring do, she held up her coffee cup to me.

"To my adventurous bestie, Emma! The very *best* musketeer!" I clinked my mug against hers, and we both laughed. "So, you going to stick around for a while?" she asked. "I could use another bridesmaid. She smiled.

"Honestly, I don't know how long I'll stay. If I'm not here, though, I promise to come back for the wedding. I'd love nothing more than to celebrate with you!" I hugged her tight. "You really are like a sister to me, Suzy. I'm so sorry I got so out of touch when I moved away." My eyes filled with a little moisture.

"Aw, honey, I understand. I do. Small town life's not for everybody. Moving off is all you ever talked about. I couldn't be surprised." She looked down at her coffee, then back up at me again. "Although, I would've thought a cute doctor would be enough to make you stick around." She winked.

"Oh, Suzy! Still trying to get your way. You're so bossy!" We both laughed.

* * *

LATER THAT EVENING, I had dinner with my grandparents, and after dinner, Snowball and I walked down to the hillside along the pasture. The night was clear and still. Beautiful purples and oranges painted the sunset, and slowly gave way to the deep blue of night.

I sat back on my palms, my feet crossed out in front of me, looking at the lights of Hillbilly Hollow twinkling in the evening sky below. I looked down toward the fort and saw the faint impression of a shape at the edge of my field of vision. I turned slightly to focus and realized it was the same apparition I had seen before. Preacher Jacob.

"Thank you for what you did," I said, unsure if he could

hear or even understand me. "I mean, with the cannonball at the fort."

I had been thinking about how that pedestal holding the cannonball mysteriously tipped forward at the perfect moment, so that the ball had knocked Teller out before he could kill me. Combined with the eerie chill I had sometimes felt while in that room, I was now convinced Preacher Jacob had been lingering in the place, and had been there at the right moment to answer my cries for help.

I continued talking to the specter. "They're putting the sword in a museum. And Teller confessed. So did Sadie. She was in on it with him. They were going to sell the sword and run off together to Costa Rica." I gave a knowing smile in his direction.

The shape came to a halt not far from me, but this time, Snowball didn't bleat or seem afraid. I patted her head.

Preacher Jacob's ghost stood upright and gave me a salute.

"Glad I could help," I said quietly.

With that, he turned and walked down toward the fort, disappearing into the ether after just a few steps.

I knew it would be the last I saw of Preacher Jacob. He could finally rest in peace. As I looked back at the sky, I thought of my parents. I wondered why I couldn't have seen them. I missed them so much. I was so little when they were killed. Would they even know me know? A single tear trickled down my cheek, then I smiled, thinking about how much they had loved me. I kissed the pads of my index and middle finger, flipping them toward the sky.

"I love you, Mom and Dad," I said.

Just then, two quick bursts of warm air blew across my face. *They know me,* I thought. *They miss me too.*

I lay back on the grass, and couldn't help but wonder if the visions would disappear with Preacher Jacob. In one way,

I hoped they would. Some *true* peace and quiet could be a very good thing. In another way, though, I was glad I had been able to see what I did. Without my – *what was it? A gift?* Well, without my abilities, I wouldn't have been able to help Tucker catch Preacher Jacob's murderer, and a killer would've gone free.

I tucked my hands behind my head and took a deep breath of the summer air. Snowball ambled over and laid her head on my belly like a pillow. The lightning bugs flew overhead, their beacons mingling with the twinkling of the stars.

Whatever was going to come my way, I believed I would be okay. If someone else needed me, whether they were alive or not, I'd help them if I could. And in the meantime, it just felt good to be home at last.

* * *

Continue following the ghostly mysteries and eccentric characters
of Hillbilly Hollow in Book 2,
"The Ghastly Ghost of Hillbilly Hollow"

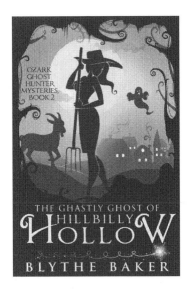

THE GHASTLY GHOST OF HILLBILLY
HOLLOW

There was always something special about summertime in
Hillbilly Hollow. Lightning bugs danced in the glow of early
evening, the smell of honeysuckle wafted through open
windows, and the flowers were in full bloom. As I drove into
town, I had the windows down in the old truck, and my
sunglasses on. The sights and smells of a country summer
filled my senses as the radio blared an old rock song and I
sang along at the top of my lungs.

I'd been back in Hillbilly Hollow for several weeks, and
was getting back into the rhythm of farm life, and enjoying
being part of the community. There were still so many things
I missed about New York, but I had forgotten how much fun
I'd had growing up in a small town. The local ice cream shop
had better ice cream than I'd ever had anywhere else. Main
Street was always festooned with lights and garlands at
Christmastime, and everyone always rallied around the local
sports teams to support the local kids. There were so many
things I had taken for granted when I was young, before
wanderlust pulled me away to the bright lights of the big city.

When I got to Main Street, signs were hanging from the

155

lampposts announcing the upcoming Hillbilly Hollow Flower Festival.

Grandpa had asked me to pick up chicken feed and some building supplies while I ran errands in town. I didn't mind running to town for this or that, or to see my friends. The distance between our farm and town had seemed like it took forever when I first got home. Now, I went to town almost every day. After all, a girl can only spend so much time on the farm with her grandparents before she starts to go a bit stir crazy.

The streets were a little busier than usual, with tourists starting to trickle in for the start of the Flower Festival. The local hotel, The Hollow Inn, was over a hundred years old, and a stagecoach stop had stood on that site before it. There was still a little restaurant on the first floor of the hotel which served breakfast and lunch. During the summer when there were lots of tourists in town for festivals and for Old Fort Days, the hotel was always full. Further out, an entrepreneurial family from St. Louis, the Shaffers, had bought the old Stephenson farm and converted it to a bed and breakfast, putting six little cottages on the property in addition to the huge, old farmhouse. The property had been featured in the Missouri tourist guide the year before and had gotten more popular since, often booking up solid in the summer.

The local feed and supply store, Farm King, was at the far end of Main Street, past the church and the walk-in clinic. Before I got that far, though, I decided I deserved to treat myself to a strawberry slush on such a beautiful summer day, so I stopped at Chapman's, the largest and newest gas station and convenience store Hillbilly Hollow had to offer.

Donna Selby was the daytime cashier at Chapman's. Her cousin Sherrie was in my class in school but Donna was a good five or six years younger, so I didn't know her as well growing up. I walked back to the slush machine and helped myself to a medium strawberry-flavored drink. Walking back up front, I took too eager a sip from the oversized straw and got brain freeze. Billy had taught me the trick of sticking my thumb against the roof of my mouth to warm up my palate. He was always full of obscure little tidbits of information like that. Being friends with the town doctor definitely had its perks.

As I got to the counter, there were a few people hanging around talking to Donna. I recognized Jasper Jenkins. His wife Ethel was one of Grandma's quilting circle friends. Lyndon Lowery was there too. He was one of the most successful farmers and land owners in town. Ted Baxter leaned on the counter across from Donna as well. He had been in our class, and Suzy told me that they had dated for a while before she reconnected with Brian, her now-fiancé. He was a nice-looking guy with blondish-brown hair and bright green eyes. Brian was more put-together, though, and his good looks were more polished. The more time I spent with Brian and Suzy together, the happier I was for her. He was a genuinely good guy, and really seemed to be in love with Suzy.

"Hello, Mr. Lowery, Mr. Jenkins. Hi, Ted. Everything alright?" I asked as I set my slush cup on the counter and put down a five-dollar bill.

"Hi, Emma," Ted said. "I guess you haven't heard, then?"

"Heard what?" I asked.

"This place was robbed last night," Mr. Lowery said in a hushed voice. "At gunpoint no less!"

"Oh, sugar! Is everyone okay?" I asked.

"Yeah, Caleb was working. Said a masked guy came right in, covered head to toe in black clothes, had a gun and a note that said 'empty the register'. He put the money in a sack and then ran out. Got away before Caleb could call the sheriff," Donna said, shaking her head. "Darn scary if you ask me."

"Probably one of these strangers in town," Mr. Jenkins said. "You know, all these tourists in from all over…no telling who's coming and going, not to mention *why* they're lurking around!"

"Wow, that's awful. Well, I'm glad Caleb's okay," I said, taking my change from Donna. "You be safe, won't you?" I gave her a concerned smile. "See you all later."

I got in my truck and headed over to the Posh Closet to see Suzy.

"Morning, Suz," I said as I walked in the door.

"Hi, Emma!" she cheerfully called from the rack of clothes she was working on.

"Bathroom," I said, putting my slush on the counter as I walked to the back.

A few minutes later, I returned.

"So did you hear," I started to ask Suzy, who was, by then, sitting behind the counter on a little stool.

"Yes! Crazy, isn't it? You don't think about an *armed robbery* someplace like this, but I guess no place is safe anymore." She shrugged.

I picked up my drink to take a sip and it was noticeably lighter than it had been when I set it down. "Did you drink my slush?" I asked her.

"Not all of it." She smirked. "Come on, Emma! You didn't bring me one," she rolled her eyes. "You left me no choice."

"*Whatever* was I *thinking?*" I said dramatically. "I will try to do better in the future!" We both laughed. "So, are you taking any extra precautions due to the robbery?"

"I don't know…I'm not sure I'd know what I could do differently," she replied.

"Maybe you should ask Tucker for some tips," I suggested.

Suzy rolled her eyes. "Or one of his deputies. Bless Tucker's heart. I'm not sure he'd be much help. When they were handing out looks and muscles, he must've gotten in the muscles line twice, and forgot he was supposed to get in the line for brains as well." We both giggled.

"Well, I'm sure you'll be alright anyway. After all, you close up by five or six most days." I looked at my watch. "Oh, look at the time. I've got a lot left to do – I'd better run."

I gave Suzy a hug around the neck.

"Text me later. Oh!" Suzy said, "Want to go to dinner later? We'll get Billy to come, too."

"Sounds good! See ya!" I waved as I walked out the door and hopped into my truck. As I put on my seatbelt, my phone buzzed. It was a text from Billy.

BILLY: Heard there was holdup at Chapman's. U coming 2 town?

I decided to hop out of my truck and walk over to the clinic instead of replying. It was only a few doors down from Suzy's shop.

Lena, the receptionist, was several years younger than us. She was married to Danny Baxter, who had taken over as preacher of the local church after Preacher Jacob was murdered.

"Hi, Lena." I smiled at the pretty redhead when I walked in. There was no one in the waiting room. "Is Bil- I mean, Dr. Will in today?" I giggled. I knew he went by Dr. Will Stone, trying to craft a more grown-up image for himself now that he was a successful doctor, but he'd only ever be Billy to Suzy and me.

Lena laughed. "Yes, Emma. He's here. Nobody's in the office – you want to head back?"

"Thanks!" I walked around the desk and to the little office he kept in the back corner.

"Yes, I am coming to town, as a matter of fact," I said, leaning against his door. "Do you suspect me of secretly being the Armed Bandit of Hillbilly Hollow?" I asked, dramatically.

"Hi, Emma," he said, a megawatt smile flashing from his tanned face. "I wouldn't put it past you, ya know. I've seen what you're capable of, after all, and am convinced nothing scares you."

"Well, almost nothing," I said, plopping down in the chair opposite his desk, and looking around at the walls of his office. They were covered with thank you cards, photos, and drawings, presumably from grateful patients. "Why'd you ask if I'd be in town today?"

"I just wanted to be sure you knew about the robbery – knew to keep your eyes peeled, that's all." He shrugged.

"Are you worried about me?" I grinned. "I should be worried about you. I mean, don't you keep some pretty high-dose baby aspirin around here?"

"Ha! Yes, if someone wants to make a killing on tongue depressors and antibacterial cream, I'm definitely in danger of being a target! We don't keep much in the way of serious medicine, and what we do have is under lock and key. It's a pretty good system. That's the great thing about the clinic, though – mostly insurance and credit cards – very little cash business."

"While I'm thinking about it, Suzy asked me to come down for dinner later. She wanted to know if you'd come too," I said.

"Yeah! That would be great!" He furrowed his brow, and cleared his throat. "I mean, that sounds cool. Whatever."

"Okay, I'd better roll. Lots to do today. Talk to you later?" I said.

"Sounds good. Be safe out there, Emma," he said in that stern, doctor-ly voice he sometimes used. I found it both extremely sweet and unbelievably dorky at the same time.

"Don't worry, I will!" I said, plucking a sucker from the jar on his desk as I left.

As I walked out to my truck, I pulled the wrapper from the sucker and stuffed the plastic into my pocket. I put the red disc against my tongue. *Mm. Strawberry!*

I heard a loud noise and my attention was pulled to the street. There were two motorcycles rolling up Main Street toward the diner. The motorcycles didn't look new – in fact, one of them looked pretty beaten up. The riders each wore a leather vest over their t-shirt and jeans, and each sported a very expensive-looking helmet. The look was a bit outdated, I thought, not to mention that it was far too hot for leather by the time the Flower Festival rolled around.

I wondered if the two bikers might be taking the scenic route from Springfield to St. Louis along old Route 66, and just stopping in town for a bite to eat. We sometimes got tourists who got off the old tourist route and came through to check out the town. It was good for business, I knew, and with so many friends and neighbors who had businesses of their own, I tried to be supportive.

I stopped at Farm King and picked up the feed for the chickens, and also picked up a couple pairs of work pants for myself. I had already ruined one pair of good jeans with barbed wire and manure, and I was determined not to lose any more of my wardrobe to farm life. Even if I was going to stick around a while, there was no point in doing farm chores in jeans that cost a hundred-fifty bucks a pair.

I also stopped at the hardware store and picked up some building materials that they had put back for Grandpa. Grandma wanted to box in the vegetable garden so the deer and rabbits didn't keep getting her vegetables. She canned fruit and vegetables, and made pickles according to the season. She put a lot of the canned goods up for us to eat, but also donated some to various fundraisers throughout the year. Her sweet pickle recipe was so good, I hesitated to eat sweet pickles made by anyone else.

The guy behind the register was younger than me, and I didn't know him well. He called for someone from the back to help me get the supplies into the truck. Before long, I was loaded up and ready to check another errand off my list.

My next stop was the Hillbilly Hollow Museum. I had to drop off some fliers from the Historical Society and wanted to give some of my business cards to Jackie Colton, Suzy's Mom who was also the museum curator. I thought she might be willing to refer anyone to me who might need graphic design work. I had known Mrs. Colton my whole life, and she had always been a supporter of my graphic design work. I knew I would find the most volume of work online, but thought it would be gratifying if I could pick up a little local business as well.

My hands were full with two big boxes of fliers for Old Fort Days as I went into the museum. I balanced the boxes cautiously as I gingerly opened the door with the tips of my fingers. As I started through the door, someone pushed past me, nearly knocking me over.

There was no mistaking her wild, silver-white mane of hair, and the multi-colored tunic she wore. It was Melody Campbell, the popular local artist. There were several pieces of her work on permanent display at the museum.

"Really, do you have to be just where I'm trying to walk? Move aside! Honestly!" She made a tsk-tsk noise against her teeth with her tongue and shook her head as she pushed me aside.

She was known for her eccentricity as much as her highly sought after paintings. Her style was a mix of impressionism and cubism, marked by bold colors and subtle design. I didn't think her work was as good as many people did, but I had been lucky enough to visit lots of museums and local galleries in New York, so I considered myself pretty spoiled in that regard.

"Hi, Ms. Campbell," I said cautiously. "Everything alright?"

"Oh, yes, it's just wonderful!" she said, rolling her eyes exaggeratedly. "My car's in the shop, and I have to walk *all the way* back to my house with *all of this*," she said, holding up two large bags of art supplies. "So yes, Emma, it's just a *wonderful* day!" She started to huff off.

"Ms. Campbell, if you'll wait for..." I started to offer to drop her at her home if she'd wait for me to leave the fliers with Mrs. Colton.

"No, I will not wait! I've told you I'm very busy. Good day!" She stormed off.

Hmpf! Rude, much? I couldn't believe I was thinking of helping that cranky woman.

I spent a few minutes with Mrs. Colton, then ran over to Founders Park. The front entrance to Founders Park was two blocks behind the Historical Society. The park was also accessible through Hollow Heights Garden via an entrance on County Road 47 at the back. It had a small playground, several benches, and a large open area that was used for festivals. Hollow Heights Garden, though, was the highlight of the park, and a source of many visitors to Hillbilly Hollow each year. It was a beautifully landscaped space, rich with examples of local flowers and plants.

Each year, the kickoff of the Flower Festival was a charity auction held on the park grounds. Local artists, both professional and amateur, created beautiful themed banners to be sold in the auction. I had promised Grandma I'd buy a pretty banner for her to hang on the front porch. She had always wanted one, but never seemed to be able to win the ones she was after at the auction.

I stopped at the registration table to pick up an auction paddle, and had just enough time to make a quick run through of the items up for sale. There were a couple of pretty banners that I thought Grandma would like. There were several nice ones with scenes of our little downtown area, and some of the natural beauty spots from around the county. Several depicted the old fort here in town, same as it stood in modern day, while others showed scenes of it in its military heyday. I came upon one banner that had pretty colors, but the abstract style wasn't my taste. I thought I recognized it as Melody Campbell's work.

As I stood, looking over the piece, someone I had yet to run into since I'd been back in town was suddenly standing beside me.

"Well, if it isn't little Emma Hooper," the tall, perfectly coiffured blonde said from behind oversized black sunglasses.

"Hello, Lisa," I replied, trying to hold back the venom in my voice. All through school, Lisa Teller, now Lisa Teller-Parks, had always seemed to get the better of me. She ended up marrying Jason Parks, local realtor, but I'd heard that they had recently gotten divorced.

She and I ended up in competition for everything. From class secretary to cheerleading – whatever I went out for, she did too, and she usually beat me. Things got really bad between us our senior year of high school. She had developed a crush on Billy, and everyone knew we were close. Apparently she was flirting with Billy, who wasn't interested, and when he rejected her, she started a hurtful rumor about us. She had told everyone in school that Billy's parents were broke, and weren't telling him, but were about to lose their house. She said that was why we were close,

Broke Billy and Little Orphan Emma. Even though none of it was true, and we'd all grown up, seeing her made my blood boil.

"I see you're looking at the Campbell banner. Looks like you finally developed decent taste after all these years. I mean, you wouldn't know it looking at your clothes." She smirked.

"You know, I hear you've made Jason a very happy man." I smiled at her.

"We're…divorced, actually," she replied, lifting her nose in the air.

"I know. That's what I meant. Enjoy the auction!" I giggled as I walked off to take my spot.

I didn't win the first banner I bid on. It was a pretty garden scene with hydrangeas all over it. Prudence Huffler was bidding on it, and I didn't have the heart to outbid her after all she'd been through with losing Preacher Jacob just a few months before. I couldn't say that Prudence looked happy, exactly, but she definitely looked better than she had during her darkest days.

The abstract banner came up, and Lisa immediately bid.

"Fifteen," she said, holding up her paddle nonchalantly.

Someone off to the side offered twenty.

"Twenty-five," I countered.

"Thirty," Lisa said.

"Thirty-five," I replied. Most of the banners had gone for between twenty and fifty dollars, so the auctioneer, Mayor Bigsby himself, was growing excited.

"Forty-five!" Lisa said authoritatively.

"Fifty!" I countered.

Another hand went up somewhere in the crowd, and Mayor Bigsby pointed, yelling, "Sixty," but never took his eyes off of Lisa and me. He had spent enough time at auctions to know a bidding war when he saw one.

"Seventy-five dollars!" Lisa shouted, holding her paddle high. The crowd grew quiet.

I chuckled. "One hundred dollars!" I replied. There was an audible gasp.

Mayor Bigsby looked at Lisa, who shook her head back and forth.

"Sold, to Emma Hooper for one hundred dollars! Emma, thank you for being such a generous supporter of the Historical Society!" Mayor Bigsby said.

I smiled and nodded graciously. *Well, crap!* I thought, *that wasn't even the banner I wanted, and I sure didn't mean to pay a hundred bucks for it!* I just hadn't wanted to see Lisa win.

I paid for my purchase and headed back toward the main entrance. The banner was more expensive than I had intended, but it was a pretty color combination, and would look nice hanging on our front porch. Besides, the money did go to a good cause and Grandma would just be happy to have a piece of artwork of her very own.

As I started walking back to the truck with my purchase, Jerry Langston, the local veterinarian, chased me down. "Emma! Emma!" he said, as he jogged up to meet me.

"Hi, Dr. Langston. Everything okay?" I asked.

"Yes, yes!" he snapped impatiently. "I need that banner." He dug into his pocket and retrieved his wallet, opening it and digging through the cash inside. "How much did you pay for it?" he asked.

"Excuse me?" I asked incredulously.

"You heard me. How much did you *pay* for it?" He pulled a few twenties from the wallet.

"Dr. Langston, this is mine, I…" I started to protest, and he cut me off.

"*Hmpf!* Alright, then! I'll give you twenty over the asking price and not a penny more! Here!" He shoved a handful of bills at me, and went to grab the banner.

I was incensed! The banner was hideous, true enough, but the colors were nice, and there was something strangely familiar about it. Almost comforting in a way I couldn't explain. It was for my grandma, and there was no way I was going to let someone take it from me.

"No, sir!" I pushed back on his fistful of cash. "This is for my grandma, and I'm taking it home to her now. Good day, Dr. Langston."

I pushed past him and headed toward my truck. I could've sworn I heard an almost growling sound as I walked away.

As I drove home, I couldn't help but wonder again about the robbery that was the talk of the town. Hillbilly Hollow wasn't that close to the interstate. It was the type of place you had to make an effort to come visit. I couldn't believe some random criminal would go out of their way to come to our little town to rob a gas station. At the same time, if it wasn't a stranger, it had to be someone local. There were a few unsavory characters that hung out at Happy Hills, the trailer park out past the junkyard on the far outskirts of town. Still, I couldn't imagine anyone being so brazen as to risk being seen and caught.

I wondered if the robbery had everyone else in town on edge too. Lisa had been in rare form today, even for her. I felt a twinge of regret at making fun of her divorce, but after all, she had been really hateful to Billy and me when we were kids, so maybe she deserved it. Melody Campbell had shocked me with her rudeness too, and for no apparent reason. I should've probably chased her down to make her let me drive her home. She lived a good distance out at the edge of town, and she wasn't a young woman anymore. Still, you can't help someone who doesn't want to be helped, I supposed.

Dr. Langston was another piece of work. I couldn't think why in the world he would expect me to give up the banner I had *just* bid to win. Of course, he clearly didn't know how much I had overpaid for it, but still, it was rude of him to try to take it from me so forcefully.

The Flower Festival was supposed to be a fun time – one of the best weeks to be in Hillbilly Hollow. This year felt different, though. I wasn't sure if it was the fog of Preacher Jacob's death a few months before, or something else, but it was as if there was something in the air in Hillbilly Hollow. Whatever it was, I didn't like it one bit.

END OF EXCERPT

ABOUT THE AUTHOR

Blythe Baker is a thirty-something bottle redhead from the South Central part of the country. When she's not slinging words and creating new worlds and characters, she's acting as chauffeur to her children and head groomer to her household of beloved pets.

Blythe enjoys long walks with her dog on sweaty days, grubbing in her flower garden, cooking, and ruthlessly de-cluttering her overcrowded home. She also likes binge-watching mystery shows on TV and burying herself in books about murder.

To learn more about Blythe, visit her website and sign up for her newsletter at www.blythebaker.com